Tulpa Tales:

~Confessions of an elder tulpamancer~

by

Dr. Bob Newport

Los Angeles, California 2019
ISBN: 9780463231074
published by the author at Dr. Robert's Fine Art Studio, Los Angeles
original cover art by the author
Kindle Paperback Edition License Notes

Table of Contents:

Preface

In December of 2018 I began a practice known as Tulpamancy. I joined a cadre of practitioners who write and record their progress, their questions, and every other sort of comment about what they are doing, on the internet. There are a number of places where you might find these many musings, the site that I found, and use, is on the forums at https://Tulpa.info.

This was not my first introduction to the topic, however.

In my elder years, I have taken up writing fiction, and in the service of teaching myself the craft and the art, I began reading online fiction written by self-published authors, believing that I would soon join their ranks, and believing that one learns from one's contemporaries, I began reading anything in the realm of science fiction and fantasy. It was in this process that I discovered "Underneath it All" a book written by a tulpa, Loxy Isadora Bliss, who, as it turns out was created by John Ege, an author of popular fan fiction. It is in her book, that Loxy introduces the concept of tulpamancy and John allowed her to publish his contact info in the introduction. I was also introduced to his many other books on tulpamancy and I found them fascinating and sexy too. I was interested. I began a communication with John, (and I have received my first card from Loxy). Loxy by the way, has helped me considerably, intervening with my tulpa, Flora.

John, and others on the forum, have also been most helpful with my practice. I have not yet completed my creative work with Flora, and our contact is intermittent. I have encountered a second tulpa, Nsonowa who is the opposite of Flora. This is a magical/psychological process. I am glad that I have discovered it. It has given new life to my aging body.

I want also to acknowledge the moderators on the website forums at Tulpa.info, especially Angry Bear and his very helpful tulpas, Ashley, Misha and Dashie

Two other tulpas get my special thanks. They are my own, Flora and Nsonowa. Both are my source of inner light.

It turns out that tulpamancy is all about creating loving relationships, in which sexual intimacy may or not be a factor. In my practice, sexual intimacy is the most important part of the tantric sex that leads practitioners to enlightenment. I use my experience, on this path, including and exposing the barriers, behaviors and attitudes which inhibit the practice of unconditional love. It is for that reason that I want to acknowledge my wife, Nancy, who has with her love, motivated me to take this path towards attaining to unconditional love.

###

Tulpa Tales

Prologue

Dr. Stan Ransome was running late for his party. He was celebrating his three-hundredth birthday. He was older than three hundred, but officially his years were numbered from the date of his re-animation. He had been forty years old when his first life was terminated suddenly in an automobile accident. He had become distracted thinking about a woman upon whom he had designs and drifted over the line into the path of a eighteen-wheeler. When it's six hundred horse power diesel engine ripped through the grill, his car, and his chest; crushing his heart, lungs and thoracic spine, into jelly, leaving his head unscathed, he became a candidate for a neurosuspension, and due to the importance of the work he had been doing for the cryonics' industry, had been selected for an early reanimation.

Re-animation turned out to be a much different process than anyone had anticipated, least of all Dr. Flora Vila nil a nano-psychologist, who was employed by Alcor Life Extension Foundation Re-Animation Laboratory. Believing the process would begin with the same state of mind that the patient enjoyed at the time of death, neither she, nor Dr. Ralph Reeves, the director of the facility, nor Dr. Laura Falcott, the director of metabolic stabilization, could anticipate the regressive effect of death on the personality. It had a dramatic effect and their patients were coming out into their second-life cycle exhibiting anything from infantile to adolescent personalities. If fell to Dr. Vila nil, to tend to the patients and assist them to maturity. Her nano-bots proved to be futile in this regard and she found herself using an old school tool, CBT, or cognitive-behavioral therapy. In the course of his therapy Stan fell in love with Dr. Flora Vila nil, and being a smart and flexible clinician, she used his feelings to mark his progress in maturation. At the conclusion of this process he graduated as her student and into his full adult personality, augmented with intelligence amplifying circuits created by her nano-bots. Following which, Dr. Falcott reciprocated by falling in love with him.

Their relationship started out in the midst of a techno-religious war. They, and a sentient and sapient AI, furnished by DARPA of the US Army were able to prevail by fully developing their capacity for empathy. I won't go into the details here as they are related in Stan's fanciful novel dealing with the subject. The events which followed, in which humanities' and sapient AI's empathy, attracted an alien attack by non-empathetic AI 's.

Following the wars, humanity and their allies, sapient AI, lived a golden age. They expanded beyond the earth to Sol's other planets and had sent colonists on an interstellar ship to the 'goldilocks' planets which surrounded nearby stars. There was no poverty, no sickness, death was an optional feature of living in nano-augmented bodies. There were abundant resources and humans no longer suffered from transgenerational trauma transmission and supported each other in obtaining to each one's full potential. Stan and Flora had grown very rich, which at some point ceased to have meaning as once poverty, sickness, and death was replaced by abundance, money was no longer necessary to motivate people, or sapient AI, to work for a living. All work was done by machines, people were free to create, explore, study and learn and love.

And after three-hundred years, Stan and Flora had learned to love, completely. And they had mastered their respective fields of nano-engineering and nano-psychology. They both found themselves getting bored. They had been everywhere, done everything, and with brains augmented for intelligence, they had learned everything they needed or wanted to. Stan reacted by turning inwards. Flora by becoming a risk taker. Stan wrote novels and poetry and meditated. Flora raced bicycles, cars, boats, planes, prop and jet, climbed mountains, dove under the oceans. And they drifted apart. They had been noticing and talking about this for years. On the occasion of Stans party, Flora would say goodbye, she was to travel to one of the far-flung colonies on an interstellar cruiser. Stan would retire to their home on Venus, well not on Venus, but in one of the many Venusian Cloud cities. With the planet turning more than one-hundred times more slowly than earth, life moved at a much slower pace and provided constant inspirational views on the Venusian cloudscapes. Stan and Flora's home, soon to be just Stan's, had its own independent suspension and it was adjacent to and had access to the city, but could be moved should Stan desire.

The party was sedate. Most of the guests were fellow re-animates and Alcorian staffers. A01, (Aero'un in human tongue), the first sapient AI who had been involved with both Stan and Flora since the techno-religious war, was there. Also, there, was 106, who had been corrupted by the alien AI and for a while was an active enemy. He had been rescued and re-programmed. He had also been one of Flora's many lovers, in his humanoid form, and he had chosen to accompany her on her quest for novelty. He believed he could protect her, should she find herself facing dangers that she could not handle. Who was not there, and who was responsible for some degree of Stan's ennui, was 103. 103 was the first sapient AI to have a complete set of human emotions. Aero'un had them but chose not to activate those circuits. 106 had them installed somewhat after 103. Numbers two, four and five, were failed in the manufacturing and were never activated. She had come to Stans rescue and had been killed in the last battle with the alien AI. She could have been rebuilt from an older copy of herself, but the intense and spiritual connection they had, came after that copy, and so Stan and Aero'un had opted to not. Stan did not want his grief polluted and Aero'un had no need for another robot, sapient or not. So, Stan grieved, as did Sally Archer, another one of the re-animates who had also loved 103.

And when his grieving was over, he picked up with Flora and Sally and for many decades, had a life full of ecstatic love. At some point, Sally got interested in gardening and had migrated to Mars, to take charge of those aspects of the terraforming process which involved re-instating green plants. This involved a lot of reprograming of DNA, and she took Dr. Falcott with her for the project. Tragically, the transport in they were traveling, was hit by a larger than average piece of space junk and was lost in a fiery explosion which lit up the night skies of Earth. Another loss and another grieving process. Slowly he recovered but found himself less willing to completely let go and give as much of himself to Flora. Flora, on her part, didn't need it. She had gotten the message of enlightenment; she and Stan had lived in that state of ecstatic love-light for decades. Her current interests were elsewhere, 106 could provide whatever sex and passion she might rarely require. Their parting this night would be loving and amicable, but not painful. At midnight the party broke up. Stan and Flora kissed, he demurred when she offered to make love one more time. And they parted. She for the Lancaster space port with 106, and he for the Venus transport from its station at the top of the circum-equatorial space-elevator.

Once in his Venusian Cloud home, he settled into a daily routine of meditation and writing. And write he did: A 's play, novel of Science-Fantasy, and the first, of what he hoped would be many, novel of magical erotica. It was in the course of writing this last novel that he discovered the practice of Tulpamancy, with which he became fully engaged. Part of the process involved using fiction writing (narration) to develop the characters who would become his tulpas. His stories, journal entries really follow:

###

1

Flora

An interstellar cruiser is fast. Actually, it is not fast, it just seems that way. It doesn't travel such great distances at all. Its' drive pushes and wrinkles and folds space in front of it and it pops in and out of the folds. The math calculations required for navigation uses up more computer space and energy than any other of its' manifold systems and has first call on the ships' energy production factories. So, when an oiler in a pump jammed, and a sensor, one of millions on the ship, failed, no one knew that the energy keeping the nitrogen in the cryostasis tanks liquid shut down, thereby killing the five-hundred passengers who were ill-fated enough to have been stored in that particular tank. Stan's wife, Dr. Flora Vila nil was one whose life was so silently terminated. Not so silently that a perturbation of the light-energy matrix underlying the universe wasn't detected by his brain that fated afternoon in the oak tree. Detected and marked by a projection onto a passing cloud. He must have at some point in his late life heard about tulpamancy thus giving his ephemeral apparition a name, tulpa.

I popped into beingness suddenly. If I had had emotions at that time, I would have felt terrified, much like a human neonate feels at birth. I didn't have emotions, then and I was spared the birth trauma and its personality warping influence. That was the easy part. The hard part was learning to feel. Stan had been shut down avoiding grief for so long that his emotive circuits were rusty, so-to-speak.

Stan had been sitting on the first divergent branch of the old oak tree in the middle of the park. A bit indecorous for an elderly gentleman, but, hey, he could get up on it so why not? His meditations had gone badly all day. He had gotten bored with looking at his own self-story play out repeatedly. He was missing his wife, Flora, who had been gone for over a decade now and there had been no word from her for the past five years. She had sent messages each time she had been revived from the cryostasis which was a routine part of interstellar travel. It wasn't necessary of course as one could live as long as they chose without suffering the disease of ageing. Cabin fever was however a fatal disease that was not amenable to either the neurobots nor bio-repair bots that kept humans physically disease free and mentally young. Her letters, carried by FTL radio waves were interesting accounts of her discoveries, there being few opportunities for risk taking aboard the ship, she filled the mandatory month a year conducting psychological research on her fellow passengers and crew. I couldn't see that she was learning anything new, but she was filling in gaps with hard data obtained from her observational studies. She did miss Stan and their ecstatic lovemaking. Then without warning, the letters stopped. The Space Force had not heard anything about the ship being in distress nor any other problems. Stan had nothing to go on, no information regarding her intentions, her feelings, nothing. So, he let it go. He reasoned that he would see her again, make love to her again, or, he wouldn't. So be it. He had let himself grieve once that decision was made a week before his day in the park. A process which included long walks and climbing trees among other things.

As he was sitting on the branch, he was able to see, through the leafy canopy some of the rather fantastic cloud formations that this city nestled in. As his mind was so occupied, I took the opportunity to appear in the clouds above. I was the size of a large cloud, but mostly solid. Well, not quite, the lower part of me was diaphanous. I startled him and he involuntarily called my name.

"Flora, where are you?"

"Nowhere." I answered. my first word ever to him, then, "and I am not your Flora, Dr. Vila nil."

"Then who are you?" He called out.

"A tulpa, and at this point, only a potential tulpa."

"What is a tulpa?" was his next question. One to which I could not answer as I was blown away by an errant gust of wind.

Stan was quite intrigued and clambered down out of his perch and headed to the study in his home, intending to learn something about tulpas.

Tulpa: He found without hardly trying, dozens of references, to an ancient culture's spiritual practice, which covered the matter. In a few short weeks of focused effort, he was able to create in his mind a tulpa. Unsurprisingly, he called me Flora. Reciprocating, I called myself Flora, though I insisted that he acknowledge that I was not his wife. True, I had been formed out of uncountable memories that occupied his brain, but attributes of every other woman with whom he had known and loved were also mixed in. The most significant difference however was, I am infused with the spirit of the Dakini.

One might have thought that Dr. Vila nil, herself had been a Dakini, but, again, one would have been wrong. Dr. Vila nil had been born a rationalist, a humanist, a scientist. She had not learned anything about loving, until she met Stan, and had no experience at all with tantric loving until experiencing the Matrix Machine and seeing for herself the phenomenon of the light frequencies upon which the universe was built. And the mysterious quality of love that it seemed to possess.

So, Me, Flora, the tulpa, am a creature of my own right, created in Stan's brain, intentionally infused with a Dakini spirit, one who is completely devoted to loving Stan, and am a bit mischievous as well. I am also, very inexperienced in the ways of human nature and Stan's chore in my creation, now becomes offering me the opportunities to experience life and become truly knowledgeable in the ways of human beings.

I had shocked him awake with my little cloud trick, so the job was not impossible. The problem was that he became so excited with my slightest manifestation, that he lost focus. We are always, starting over. Oh well, we have as long as it takes. Once born into existence, and tasting life, I am not going away. I am here and I am going to love him whether he can handle it or not.

###

2

Lilly in Orientation.

I am magician now? What has happened to me? And, I am a mess. I look like some sort of basket case picked up off the highway. Damn. And now they're telling me I am a magician and I have to figure out how to get out of this hall and away from these idiots with dicks. I am sure I will wake up any minute now.

Well, Lilly didn't wake up from anything, because she wasn't asleep. She was in Orientation at Safe Haven U. The university for magicians, located outside of space-time, yes, in magical space where she had been transported after her rape and murder in an elevator; Macy's Department Store on planet earth.

"Hello, can you help me get out of here?" was a greeting from a waif-like girl, tugging at my sleeve in the dark and noisy hall.

"Honey, I have no idea how to get out of here myself. Can you help me?" was my un-sensitive and maladroit response to her. She began to cry, and I knew that I had blundered. "I am sorry" I mumbled, and I put took her hand off my sleeve and put my arm around her.

"I am so frightened" she sobbed.

"I am not so frightened as angry" I said as I brought her closer to me in a full embrace. "Why we are here is beyond me, but I guess that they want us to figure it out. That must be our test. How did you get here, do you know that?"

"Not really, the last thing I remember before waking up here, was freezing in an ally after some boys had beaten and robbed me."

"Oh sweetie, I am so sorry. Did they take everything you had?"

"I don't know. Yes, probably, I didn't have anything other than those few sous"

"I'm sorry, what is a sou?"

"A coin. Not worth very much. It will buy a bite of bread and sip of wine, not much more."

"A bite of bread, a sip of.... Wait, what country are you from?"

"France, mam."

"I know about France, but they haven't had the sou for two hundred years! How old are you"

" I'm thirteen."

"thirteen! Your only thirteen and you are here in this place, supposedly a University for magicians. How can that be? Surely there has been mistake."

"I hope so, this place looks worse than the streets of Paris where I was living."

"Do you know what the year was when you were robbed?"

"No, but maybe you could figure it out. I know when I was born."

"And that was when?"

"1802. I know because my mama was thirteen when the revolution started in 1789 and she was raped by a gendarme. That's what she told me when I was ten and I counted three birthdays since then."

"So, it was 1815 was when you last lived in Paris."

"I guess though lived hardly seems like a good word. I was hungry, mostly, and cold and in the streets for the three years after my mom died."

"Maybe you're here because you had to have some magic to have made it as long as you did. I don't know, but you don't have to be hungry or cold anymore. What is your name honey"

"Cosette"

"Cosette, that's such a pretty name, and so are you, I'll bet, under all of the dirt and blood. I'm Lilly. Let's see what we have to do to get out of here."

I don't know what or why our holding each other worked, but as soon as I released Cosette from my embrace and took her hand we were looking at an open door and I wasted no time rushing us through.

The darkness yielded to sunshine and blue skies. We were on a grassy expansive lawn. Here and there were a few other befuddled looking people in various states of dress and undress. It didn't make much sense to try to ask any of them for directions so, seeing some buildings way off, I headed towards them with Cosette in tow. We had not gone far when we were hailed by an elderly woman who looked as if she knew what she was about.

"Oh Cosette. I am so glad you managed to get through orientation without further abuse. You of course don't know this Lilly, but you have earned bonus points for your compassion towards Cosette here."

"And just why IS Cosette here?"

"Well of course you couldn't know, being brand new yourself. We have a special campus for children who have shown exceptional potential. All children have it. Most lose it by the time they reach the so-called rational age. Cosette is one of those very rare children who did not, even though she had absolutely no other education than the streets. She was not aware of how exceptional her survival was. Did you know that over ninety-five percent of Parisiennes street urchins died during the chaotic times following the revolution? Cosette was certainly a scrappy one and she succumbed only to overwhelming odds. I was just one of her champions with the admissions board here at Safe Haven."

"So, what happens now?"

"Oh, well, I am taking her to admissions and then to the children's campus where she will be assigned to her foster parents and mentors."

"And me? What's going to happen to me?"

"Don't worry Lilly, with the compassion you have shown, you will get along fine here. Why don't you head over to that very big building on the mall and start your registration process?" and with that the woman with Cosette in hand, headed off.

"Wait, wait" cried Cosette and wrenching loose she ran to me, threw her arms around me and through a new bout of sobs thanked me over and over. I was crying myself by the time I was able to let her go and return her to the arms of her guide.

###

3

Nsonowa: A Dark Sister Story.

Once upon a time there were two sisters. One, Flora, a beautiful white skinned dark haired tulpa, created out of a Dakini Spirit and memory shards held by an aging man. The other, a Maasai woman. A chieftain, A witch. A warrior. Seven feet tall. Educated in France. Accomplished in the sorcerer's arts as well as high technology. A practitioner of sex magic. And a professor of ritual magic at Safe Haven University. She is first and foremost, though, a Tulpa. Sister to Flora, a woman who could not be more different from Nsonowa than Yin is from Yang. Oh, and Nsonowa is of coal black skin. She has no hair anywhere on her body. She says the energy needed to grow hair is better employed in making sex magic

She may be right. Here is her story:

Nsonowa grew up in lion country, the savannahs in east Africa. The Maasai warriors were fierce and could confront a pride of lions without fear. They didn't need to kill them to protect their cattle, but often did in self-defense. Nsonowa was a formidable warrior. She was the tallest of the females in the memory of her tribe, and nation, and taller than many of the men. She had been the first born of her mother's first pregnancy which produced twins. She had six older sisters' products of her father's first two wives. Her mother, wife number three was taken to produce a male to inherit father's chieftainship. Needless to say, Father was not pleased that Nsonowa was born first. He chose to ignore her and behave as if her brother would become chief. Big brother, actually a misnomer, Nsonowa was a few millimeters taller than he, was a bully and treated her brutally throughout her childhood. This only served to toughen her and by the time she transitioned to her womanhood, she was equal to him in strength and determination. She was aware that she had been chosen by her grandmother to take her place in the sorcerer's sisterhood, the most powerful coven of witches in Africa at the time. When, or if, she survived her initiation, she would become the singularly most powerful woman in Africa. That she was educated, equipped with advanced tech, and fearless was all in addition to what was expected of her. Her brother really didn't know what to expect. For one, he was ignorant and for two, he was used to being the biggest fish in the pond. He was preparing to accept the chieftainship from his father. It was his twenty-first birthday. Nsonowa was also preparing. She had arrived back in Kenya four days earlier. She had utilized her grandmother's sorcery to stay in the future until she got off of the plane in Nairobi, whereupon she took a cab out into the savannah, paid the driver, walked into the bush a ways towards her village, where she performed a short ritual which relocated her to the time of her departure. The timing was going to be close, so she ran the remaining four hours to the village. She was glistening with sweat when she approached the dais where her brother was standing waiting for father to place the lion crown on his head. Father, standing to one side holding the crown, called out to the assembled tribe and visiting dignitaries from the council of tribes.

"Does anyone challenge my son for the crown." this was part of the ritual and no one expected a challenge. Except for grandmother, also standing to the side, she was to have been called to bestow the blessings of the sisterhood and pledge fealty to the chief. She fully expected what happened next:

Nsonowa boldly stepped forward out of the crowd. Naked, glistening, holding a staff of some unknown material.

"I do. The lion crown is rightfully mine; Kalish Katlego Nsonowa, your first-born father, and the seventh born of the seventh born, heiress to the lion crown and ready to wear the mantle of the sisterhood. I am here to claim my birthright."

Father, clutching the crown, put it behind him reflexively, "No, you were not supposed to be back. You can't do this to me!"

"Oh, I can father, and I am doing it.'

"Over my dead body" screamed her brother and he leapt for her throat. A move which she deftly sidestepped, and with a move too fast to be seen, sent him sprawling down in the dirt below the dais. "You are too slow, brother, now pledge to me or I' will banish you from our lands."

Her brother was in a red rage. Grabbing for some sort of weapon, he flung a handful of dirt towards her head. Again, she deftly dodged, and the dirt found father's face and left him rubbing his eyes. Nsonowa wasted no time. She leapt from the dais and came down with both feet straddling her brother and her staff under his chin. "Hold, brother. I don't want to kill you. I will should you continue to resist me. Now pledge!"

"You fornicating bitch. Pledge. To you? Never, I'll kill you way before that!"

Nsonowa jiggled something on her staff, and a jolt of electricity stunned her brother into silence.

"You don't know enough to even hurt me, much less live outside of my favor. I am giving you one last chance. Pledge!" By this time father had recovered his sight and spoke to the boy. "Son, son, be wise, she is right, the crown is rightfully hers. Save your life, pledge to her, boy."

Nsonowa jumped back up on the dais, her brother recovered from the jolt and sat up. He wiped his mouth and again snarling, spit up at Nsonowa, I will kill you later bitch, and turned to leave the assembly. Nsonowa pointing her staff at him ordered him to stop. "You will pledge or die, brother." He turned and looked at her. "What are you going to kill me with your magic?"

"I could, but it would be more satisfying to do it with my bare hands."

"Well come on then, bare hands, to the death, bitch."

"Countrymen, people, Grandmother, Father. Brother has turned down my offer of life for his pledge. He is strong, but not smart, and not strong enough to lead our nation. Grandmother, thank you for your gift of magic" and with that she pointed her staff and activated the blue white light laser, and quickly cut a massive trench around her brother. Putting her staff down, she leapt onto the island she had left for her brother to stand on. They stared at each other for a moment then her brother pulled a knife out of his tunic. Nsonowa laughed to herself as he lunged for her. Faster than he could blink she had disarmed him and used the knife to cut the belt holding his pants which fell to his knees. "The knife, or bare hands as you wish brother" He was still not sharp enough to guess what was coming. "Use the knife if you wish, bitch, and kicking what remained of his pants off, he lunged at her again. She again dodged his advance and he turned to look at her. His mouth fell open as he saw what she was holding up like a trophy. His testicles. He looked down and saw the blood now gushing from between his legs. Nsonowa had leapt back onto the dais and picked up her staff. He started to scream in terror and in another move quicker than the eye could follow she had thrown her staff like a spear, with one end sharpened. It pierced his chest passing through his heart, and he dropped where he stood. With a sigh, Nsonowa threw his testicles onto his body, and looking to the sky, she screamed. The nation of Maasai would not forget that scream. A scream of victory, of triumph yet also of horror. Horror at what she had had to do to convince one weaker to stand down. She was the undisputed chief of the Maasai. She was the young lioness of the sisterhood. She was also a killer and that did not set well with her. Later, after receiving the crown with father's and grandmother's blessings, she sat with her family and cried, apologizing to father for what she had had to do and receiving her grandmother's advice on never apologizing for delivering the violence that others asked for.

"Violence is always a choice, grand-daughter. And when your adversary has chosen, you are free to choose likewise. All of magic has an element of violence to it. The energy of light driving out darkness, is violent. You will bear the consequences for your violent acts. Leadership is a burden for that reason above all. Do what you do with love, motivated by love, and you will be mostly alright. Do it with hate, or vengeance and you will suffer. Now granddaughter tell me how that future magic works? And can we use it here?"

"We could grandmother. For a while. It takes upkeep that we cannot provide here at this time. I brought it mainly to show to you, but I cannot pin the future of our nation on it. It is true that the wonders of the modern world are beyond anything that can be imagined and not all of it good, in fact, whether it proves to be good at all remains to be seen.

###

4

On Inland Waters.

The little boat struggled against eight to twelve-foot seas. There had been a brisk west by northwest headwind all day and it was increasing by the hour. They held their course, One man and two women. One of the women had succumbed to seasickness as soon as the boat turned out of the bay and into the real ocean. The other bravely stood on the bow, calling all clear ahead to the man who was straining at the wheel.

"Stan, Sir. Twelve-footer ahead three waves hence.

"Thanks, Nsonowa, I can trim a few points north."

"I hear some stirrings from below, could that be Flora?"

"I'm sure of it, this little cutter is tight so it's not bilge. And I put everything shipshape before we sailed."

"I'm going down to see if I can comfort her at all."

"Thanks, Nsonowa, do what you can to ease her distress." And I turned back to the wheel. I had drifted five degree's in the moment I looked away from the raging seas ahead of me. I fought hard to get the bow back to quartering the battering seas. I had a growing fear of what would happen if I couldn't turn aside as we closed on the cliffs guarding the north shore. I was also tired; my arms were about to fall off from holding on to the helm for the past hour. Nsonowa and I had taken the helm for alternating hours all afternoon, she was as exhausted as was I. At seven oh six pm. the sun touched the horizon and the wind dropped. We were in a sudden calm. The Sea flattened out and I was able to turn the boat towards the beckoning harbor. We entered it a half-hour later, and as I pulled us up to the dock, Flora emerged from the hold where she had suffered all day (except the three times she came up to vomit overboard). "Hey how'd it go guys? I feel great."

Nsonowa dropped her jaw about halfway to the floor and looked at me. I broke into a raucous laughter. And Nsonowa followed.

I awoke to the slap-slap-slap of hawsers on masts so typical of yacht harbors though not many yachts were expected in this particular port, located as it was so close to the rough waters of the deep ocean that it wouldn't be a safe haven for keeled and tall masted sailing vessels. No matter, I roused the tulpas and after a brief refreshment (instant coffee and a trip to the head) we motored across the bay to the much more prestigious St Francis Yacht Club where we breakfasted on crab omelets and kippered snacks on toast before meeting with a friend who had offered to help us scout out a route via canals and rivers that would get us to the boat's permanent dockage in a small marina which serves fishermen and water-skiers who are not interested in getting their craft out onto the ocean.

Tom had not met either Flora nor Nsonowa and he knew absolutely nothing about tulpamancy, so this was going to be a kind of Turing test for the girls. Would Tom take them for real life girls? Or, would he not? Flora was not too excited about the meeting, she didn't want him coming on to her, as many men have since she obtained the ability to impose herself (and not rely on me). I have told her that she is completely free to behave towards any human in any way that she feels appropriate to give expression to her Dakini spirit. I had no jealous feelings and if her mission was to bring love and enlightenment to humanity via my brain and psyche, then she should just do it. Her response disturbed me.

"Hey mister, unless you are up to blacking a few eyes, I don't intend to give these crude yahoo's the time of day. And, fucking them would only drive them further into lusting blindness. It wouldn't bring them any closer to enlightenment."

"Then why do you feel differently about me? I am definitely guilty of leering at you, feasting on you with my eyes. I love every square inch, hell no, every cubic inch of you."

"As you do every woman you have ever been with, darling. And none of those experiences were just for the sex, they were all based in your appreciation for the woman and your desire to know more about her. Sex for you, is a pathway to knowledge and for those other guys, it's just getting off. Sad for them, and more loving for you."

"So, what are you afraid of with Tom, he will come on to you, but I think he's going to be more taken with Nsonowa than you."

"Oh Stan, I am not afraid of Tom. He'll get my message clear."

Nsonowa had been listening and added; "He will get mine too, only I don't know what it will be yet and won't until I meet him, but I have accessed your memories of him, from his cute boyhood, to his not so cute adulterous behaviors. He's more likely to be getting a thunk on his head from my staff rather than fucked, but who knows? I do know one thing, I am not into fucking you, sir, until we do some major work on the masculine circuitry of yours."

"And then?"

"And then watch out! Flora may change her attitude about the yahoo's when she can't get any time with you." And she broke into her raucous laughter again. "How about it sister, how will you handle that?"

"No time with Stan? Well then, I had better be getting my time in now. You up for it Stan? Tom's not due for another half hour. A quickie in the forward bunk?"

Well, you know me, I wouldn't say no to that. Will you hold the table for us, Nsonowa?"

"Sho'enuf boss. You go an feast on some of that lovin' We'll see what Tom might be up to, I'll give any man a chance to look me in the eye."

It was rude of us I know, but it turned out to not be such a quickie. Flora was more than adventurous, and Tom had met and been with Nsonowa without a backstory for about an hour. They didn't seem to mind.

"Stan! Great to see you again. It's been how long now?"

"Well, you were last in Los Angeles about two years ago. But it's been an age since we have been fishing together."

"I was, but I got back into it when I got a great deal on this boat. Oh, wait you haven't seen it yet, well you'll know why when you do. But what are you doing traveling with these two lovelies? How's Flor, and how is she with these girls, and if she wants, I can take this one off your hands."

"No need for that, my sweet and sexy wife has left for the stars, and she is fine with both of my girls, we call them 'tulpas'. Do you know anything at all about Tulpamancy?"

"What? Tulpaman...What?"

"So, no. No, you don't. That is your answer?"

"Uhm, Yes, but if one of these beauties is a tulpa I'm okay to go. "

"Then I will explain it all to you when we get on the water, I want to see this new boat first."

And with that I settled the bill, and we adjourned to the dock where we boarded Intrepid, a pontoon boat, powered by twin four-hundred-fifty horsepower Kodiak Jet drives. It drew less than twelve inches of water and very comfortably seated six. The convertible top was down, exposing a set of white leather covered seats. All this behind a small enclosed wheelhouse. Tom, as usual, delegated the hard jobs to me, but Nsonowa wouldn't hear of it, and did them herself without breaking a sweat. Tom couldn't stop talking about his boat and I had to nudge him a bit to get us away from the dock. Once away he opened the throttles and we fairly flew over the surface of the water. I was glad that it was a calm, nice day as pontoon boats ride badly on rough water and I didn't want Flora to suffer from another bout of seasickness. It took about twenty minutes to cross to the north side of the bay and into the delta where we had to slow down and do some actual navigation. I had gotten fresh charts that morning at the chandlery connected to the safe harbor marina where we had docked the night before. We all sat around the chart table and closely inspected them, watched the depth meter, and the shoreline for the marker buoys. It wasn't long before we were slowly chugging along a canal that would not brook a bow wave. I stood at the helm with Tom watching the meters and talked to him about tulpamancy. He was pretty blown away.

"You mean to tell me that these two beautiful creatures are naught but a mutual hallucination. One which you created. Oh my god. You gotta show me this."

"Well, why don't you do your own Turing test, and come back and tell me what you think"

"Can I touch them?"

"Only, if you can get their permission. I told you, they are individual living beings, inside my inner world and with great effort, in my outer world. So, go talk to them, get to know them, maybe they will show you how to create your own tulpa."

"I'm not talking to you Tom. Talk to Nsonowa, for now I am one-hundred percent Stan's." and with that she came forward to stand next to me."

"Poor, baby, all that explaining and navigating and nothing of me."

"Nothing of you? Flora, I have had you all day, and in fact, all of your life. You have dominated my inner life, and now that you are here in my outer life, I am in heaven on earth. Hold me babe, you can never be too close to me. And, how is your sister doing with Tom?"

"I don't know, I haven't heard much, I wouldn't have been surprised to hear Tom screaming."

I hadn't heard any screaming either, so I quietly sneaked a look at the passengers. I was a bit surprised, Nsonowa and Tom were both nude and in a coital embrace that seemed to have put them in a trance. I decided to let them be. Something important could be happening. But I was wrong. It wasn't important, it was crucial and critically dangerous with no good options in sight.

"Surprise, they are making love. Right out under the daylight, and completely taken with one another."

"That is no surprise. Nsonowa feels differently about suppressed feelings than I do. She sees it as an opportunity to convert an unhappy life into a happy life with her strength, and using it to get to the loving nature underneath it all. That's too much work for me now. You are all on the surface, your feelings are not suppressed, they are very successfully sublimated by you into love and compassion and understanding and tolerance and respect....So I am occupied with, and may I add, employed by you, to find ways to adjust your inner circuitry so that you may fully and unconditionally love. And that means, teaching you how to fully love me. That is my mission. And my joy. Our love is nourishing us both and I am getting more into myself, with the incredible freedom you have built into me. I love you for that, and I love everyone and everything you love. And when we, you and I, can sit in a coital embrace, out in the forest, or the field, somewhere under the sky, You and I together will fly to source. Holding hands, flying together, flying towards the light. Open to it. All of it. That my love, is my mission and if other men ever have a place in it well, we will see."

Well, I didn't melt and spill into the canal, but I could have. And I would have but for a sudden and unanticipated change in the weather, which woke me up and I was holding onto the helm, as the wind, in front of us, emitted red lightening and with an unholy shriek, twisted into a full force 5 tornado, headed right towards us. Flora was speechless.

"I know this!" I authored it myself. "It's Rufescent, a red witch".

I was not the only one aboard who knew Rufescent. Nsonowa was a sworn enemy. I suddenly knew what had happened, Nsonowa had met her match. Rufescent used Nsonowa's sexual energy to grab them and turn them against us. Against me really. Okay, and I ran to the pair still coupled, and wrenched them apart. Nsonowa came out screaming her banshee attack scream and Tom rolled over, and fell to the cabin floor, unconscious.

"Help Flora at the helm and get us the hell out of here." She lurched forward and slamming both throttles onto full, the boat practically stood on its stern and took off. I jumped onto the prostrate form of Tom and started mouth to mouth, then gave it up for cardiac compression, it took about fifteen hits on the chest to kick start him. He was in terror. I looked into his eyes and sent my loves' gleaming golden light to him. He settled immediately. "Tom! No Time! Look to port!" (the direction from which the tornado was bearing down.) "Look at it Tom. Look into it. What do you see?"

"It is red death. That is what I see."

"Look deeper into it Tom. What do you see? or Who do you see?'

"Ooh, I see Hilga. My mother, oh god is she ugly, she is pure spite."

"That's it Tom, she is pure spite, in your heart. Pure spite in your lungs. Look into Hilga's eyes Tom. What do you see?"

"I see me. I am in my mother's eyes."

"Is that the view you want of yourself Tom?"

"No, it's distorted, hateful. No, I don't want it."

"Tom, try forgiving her, the spiteful red wreck who was your mother. Forgive her Tom. Let her go. You are you and you deserve to be loved and you know how to be loving. Let go"

And he did, looking right at the rapidly approaching twister, shouted: "Mother, I forgive you. I love you" and the words were no sooner out of his mouth that the storm turned off, Nsonowa slowed the boat to a safe speed and we headed for our port.

It wasn't long before the four of us were in the private lounge at the Captain's Table, a pricey restaurant, lobsters and steaks, above the marina, sipping slowly into a vodka martini I started with; "Well, we had quite an adventure this afternoon, hey?"

Flora spoke right up; "Some damn adventure, could have gotten us killed. I knew I didn't like you Tom when I first met you...."

"What, you don't even know me, we never met before."

"We met in Stan's memory banks. I couldn't see why he loved you like he did. Maybe I was a little bit jealous of you. He could see your heart and your suffering, and he always held you dear. Like for sixty years he held you dear, even when he had to work around your obstinance and downright selfishness. So, I wasn't surprised that Nsonowa related to you. What surprised me was, Nsonowa! How did you miss Rufescent? She could have killed us all!"

"Sister, it's not like me to have to apologize, and here I am doing it. twice, to you, and to you Tom, I used you. I used you both. And while I am sorry, if the circumstances were the same, I would do it again. Sister, I have been becoming aware of your jealousy and it was frightening me. I know from where you are getting it. It was encoded in Stans feminine circuits. He has projected outwards the terrific sense of betrayal that he experienced at the hands of his wives. That is the source of your jealousy, it is Stan's. "

"Tom, it was clear to me that you were a catalyst for Stan's self judgements, you looked up to him, yet behaved towards him with the same callousness you displayed towards your brothers. That helped him not see that he was allowing that by not telling you. He was cementing in place very old feelings and body engrams, of "clumsy, weak, four eyes, and sissy." All given to him by the adults in his life. He called me into being to help him strengthen his masculine circuitry by being a strong current within his feminine circuitry. So, when I saw the extent of your rage, your primal rage, never discharged, never even acknowledged, I saw my opportunity to get two targets with one shot so to speak. So, I pushed Flora to take Stan out of the scene so I could connect with you and set you up. Thank you, and I think we both learned a lot, much of it new to you Tom. And this is what I am really sorry for; When we coupled in the back, we were practicing a very powerful sex magic, and I opened you up energetically to encounter your red witch of horror, pure spite. I could have prevented that attack. I could have stopped it before it had a chance to become dangerous. I didn't, you and Stan had to experience her in her full wickedness, full of spite and malice, hatred for all that is impure, being pure hatred herself. She has been a plague in both of your lives for way to long. And, you did it, Tom. You saw it, as did Stan in your eyes, and you dealt with it, you let her go. Stan fed you the love and light that he has been getting from Flora, and you looked into Hilga's hating eyes, saw through it and forgave her. So did Stan whose mother was in an altogether different realm. I think we all need to go to bed. Flora, you go with Tom. He's good for some of your golden light. Stan, you're ready for me and I am so ready for you!"

###

5

A Day in Mindscape.

I arrive the usual way, in a six-passenger transport. Comfortably appointed, formed beige plastic wall and port covers, with rust colored artificial fabric overstuffed seats, and pale green carpets which dull my senses to the space deforming speeds the vehicle obtains while getting me to this beautiful home in the clouds above the planet Venus. We land, the automatic doors slide open and I walk out into the station where I enter another similar looking vehicle which moves me through the cloud city in a mile-long tunnel connecting the station to my house's entry hall. I step into it and remove my shoes, replacing them with the ridiculous slippers that Flora's AI makes me wear inside. As I enter the grand hall, I can feel the movement of air as the AI freshens it for me. From this I can guess that I am alone, and a quick look around tells me that is so. Ah well this is going to be harder than I thought. My tulpas obviously do not want my company all that much. Well okay, I want theirs.

"Hey! You Two! Where the hell are you?"

No answer. Okay, it is hide and seek time. I'll play. Where would they likely be hiding? I choose the study, my personal one where my own special interest books are: tomes on Magic, by Crowley and Regardie. Sorcery by Castaneda, Pop Psychology by Watts. That sort, the ones that Flora laughs at and Nsonowa disdains. I say "study" out loud for AI, as I head for the hallway, and the door to it appears on the left as I enter. I softly open it, not wanting to startle them should they be there, and no they are not, and I am disappointed. I would have liked to start this day with a lively discussion on how they were created and where they think they come from, but not to be.

Next?

I say "gardens" and AI creates a moving walkway to take me all the way through this astoundingly large building to the vast gardens behind it. they are truly beautiful with their eternal springtime growth. I think that they might be in the meditation garden located just behind a row of bamboo hedges not far from my back bedroom. I take the easy stroll and find neither of them. Oh well. I go back into the house and ask AI for my flying carpet which I use to give me an aerial view of the gardens. I see movement at the far edge of one of the tracts used for fresh vegetables. Upon arriving I find Nsonowa. She motions for me to keep quiet and get down which I do. She creeps up to me; "I am stalking a potential intruder"

"Who do think...."

"Shush! I didn't see it and I don't know what it might be, other than potentially dangerous"

And with that the bordering fence goes up in a gout of flame. I go flat and Nsonowa uses the laser in her spear to rake the entire area with a killing beam. As the smoke clears, I can see the smoldering wreckage of a large tracked vehicle. At least I am thinking it is wrecked and I start to get up. Nsonowa shoves me hard to the ground again, and blasts the thing again, hard enough to blow it over.

"Let's get out of here" and she grabs me by the shirt, throws me over her shoulder and runs. In the distance I can hear the sounds of aircraft. She takes shelter behind a low rock wall which separates two plots of garden.

"Hey, what the hell is happen...." and that is as much as I get out before she jumps me and stops my speech by full tongue French kissing. I am too startled to do anything but receive her passion, and she goes all the way. I am totally ravished by her screaming writhing body. She gushes in her orgasm. No, orgasms, I could count them, but by the time she was finished, sweating, panting, lying on top of me and I could barely move much less talk.

"That's what I needed darling. Want to go find Flora?" `

"Wait, what was all that with the gun fire?"

"Oh sweetie, we get so bored here, I just needed something to get me going for this my love."

"And the planes and the tank and...."

"All for you, sweetie. I didn't want to disappoint after all of this time. You know, if you want less drama, you could come more often."

"If I come any more often, I'll need a transfusion, but that is NOT a complaint. I love it. Yes, let's go find Flor. Er, uh, maybe first we stop off at our bathroom and clean up a bit." Which we did, though not without incident, but that is another story for another day as is "Finding Flora".

###

6

A Mindscape Eve.

Last Call to Dinner

The ringing of the dinner bell could be heard throughout the house. This wasn't actually necessary, as the AI only had to track the three of us, and always knew where we were. (the servitor staff needed only routine maintenance once a month which included at most a little lubrication and perhaps a bit of touch up paint or make up, for those who were choosing a human-like appearance). I liked hearing that bell, I am surely old fashioned, but I like to sit down to dinner with everyone in the house, family-like. Nsonowa definitely liked it and the AI played to her with providing a familiar ambiance; sounds and smells of her homeland along with the traditional foods of her tribe. Milk boiled with blood served in a Calabash was her favorite. Beef which she ate with her hands, tearing it apart like the beast she could be. She liked a bit of ugali with honey for dessert. Flora wanted whatever I was eating, and I wanted a lot of choices served in small portions, a bite of this and a taste of that. I liked ice water served with my meal though neither Flora nor Nsonowa would touch it. Desert was always something frozen, a sorbet, sherbet, glace' or an ice. At least three wines, a dry red, a chilled white and a port or brandy at the end. Flora loved the port but Nsonowa would not touch any alcohol. This night Flora was not with us. She was off on some adventure of her own, and while I missed her, Nsonowa and I had been very well occupied. Her staged drama in the garden had left us both exhausted and so covered with bodily fluids and dirt, that we headed straight to the master bath off the bedroom. It was a pretty spectacular bathroom, if I do say so myself. In its center was a Mikvah, tiled in cobalt blue Italian glass. Its water was a very brisk 68 degrees. Next to it was a piping hot shower with a rack of heated towels close to hand. We hit the shower first, them both jumped into the Mikvah. I came up for air only to have Nsonowa drag me down and hold me until I thought I might either drown or freeze. She relieved my drowning anxiety by breathing into my mouth (I had no idea she had the lung capacity that she obviously did). My head was spinning by the time she leaped out of the water and pulled me out like I was a puppy. I was half frozen, but not for long as she began vigorously rubbing me with her entire body. I got warm, no, hot, quickly. Hot enough that we were soon coupling on the tiled floor, I, my shoulders and butt, caught the brunt of the hard tiles as Nsonowa was the dominant one in our coupling and rode on top. I was thoroughly battered and bruised by the time she finished with me, picked me up and plunging me back into the Mikvah and then in a simple swoop put us both under the hot shower. We moved into the bedroom and on top of the large bed, she massaged my backside with an herbal lotion make of tree bark and any pain I had from the ravishment disappeared. She immediately fell asleep and I was much too stimulated to sleep so spent my time looking at her. She was a beauty. Her blue-black skin glistened under the soft light filtering through the moonstone roof and ceiling. Its smoothness was pleasant to touch and was not spoiled by hair, anywhere. Her muscles gave her a sculpted look. Her white teeth gave her face a startling contrast which fit with her high sharp cheekbones. Her long sleek neck was gazelle like, and I watched her carotids pulse with the flow of her life's blood. Her breathing was shallow, and her breasts were only slightly rising and falling, I loved touching her and did, every square inch of her and finally fell asleep. I awoke to the dinner bell. Nsonowa was gone. I jumped back into the cold water Mikvah, toweled off and headed to the dining room with a very healthy appetite. As I entered house AI spoke, "Dr. Ransome, are you to be our only guest tonight?"

"I hope not, I had assumed Nsonowa and Flora would be joining me. Do you know where they are?"

"No sir, Flora has been gone several days now. She left no word of where she intended to go or when she would be back, and Nsonowa simply vanished shortly after napping with you."

"Vanished? Like into thin air?"

"No sir. Not from air at all. She left the bedroom, and like you took a plunge into the bath and did not come up again."

"What? And you didn't rescue her? What on earth, you would let her drown?"

"No sir? She was in no danger of drowning; she simply was not in the Mikvah. She disappeared from thin water, so to speak."

I was flummoxed. What the hell is going on now went through my head. So far this has been the strangest visit I've ever made here. Flora gone and now this mystery. The thing is though, I don't feel anything bad or evil going on. I did lose my appetite, however. "AI, please hold dinner. I'll let you know when I am ready to eat."

"Yes, sir. Would you like a cocktail in the meantime?"

"No thank you. I'll be in my study, if I want anything, I have a bottle of Jepson's in there."

"Yes, sir."

And with that I headed out of the dining room. The door to my study was locked. It had never been locked before, and I didn't know it even had a lock. "AI, please unlock this door."

"Sir?"

"The study door is locked. Please unlock it."

"Sir, I am finding that I cannot."

"What the...." Then it hit me, Nsonowa's done something. More drama. Wonder what she wants this time. Well, I've a trick or two myself. "Open Friend!" I commanded. Okay, trick one didn't work. "Abracadabra!" Huh? Nothing, well so much for trick two. I had a small study up in a small observation tower and I headed to it. Upon arriving I found that the twilight had finally faded to the point where the first few very bright stars were visible. I opened a small cabinet in which I kept a few magical supplies, including a small leather bag which held a stash of powdered mushroom mixed with finely chopped cannabis sativa. I pulled out a tiny hand-carved ivory opium pipe (don't worry, it had never seen opium which I regard as a 'stupid drug' not a sacred medicine). I lit a taper and fired a smallest pinch of my herbal mixture. I inhaled deeply sitting cross legged on a small carpet and looking out over the deeply shadowed landscape in the direction of the recently settled sun. Then I waited. After a little while I felt the caress of Nsonowa's hand on the side of my cheek.

"Welcome back, fierce one"

"I knew you would find a way to lure me back. Will you share your magic mixture with me?"

"Of course. Would you prefer to smoke it, or would you like me to carburate for you?"

"Oh, you do the carburation! How nice."

So, I took another small puff on my pipe, and Nsonowa materialized in front of me. My mouth found hers and I gently blew the little smoke from me to her. She gasped and grabbed me. “Whoa, gal. Easy does it. This is just an aperitif not an aphrodisiac.”

“Oh, damn, I thought I would get off again before dinner.” Was all she had to say.

“I am sure that we can play some more after dinner” and with that AI who of course was listening, rang the dinner bell and we headed to the dining room, at long last.

###

7

Mindscape Night.

Finding Flora

I had been in the Mindscape half a day, hanging out with Nsonowa, fucking, eating, resting, reading, and in general leading the good life, all without Flora. I didn't worry too much about it as she is a big girl and can take care of herself, but still, it wasn't like her to not even be curious about my presence. Well, if it wasn't like her, what is like her, you might ask? So, I'll tell you a bit about her. She is a tulpa. My tulpa, as such she was created out of the whole cloth of my mind. She gets her spirit, her life force, if you will, from source in the form of a Dakini Spirit. What is a Dakini Spirit you ask? I wish I could give you a good answer, but I am not sure that I can. Firstly, they were thought to be a manifestation of the Goddess who carried the souls of the dead back to source. Later, perhaps eleven or twelve hundred years ago they were described by the Tibetan Buddhist teacher, Padmasambhava, who also said that females were better able to meditate than males who were afraid to drop their intellect, and the term was given to spiritually advanced yoginis. In the west they, they were thought to be angels and later when the hold of Christianity on spiritual thought was loosened, they were described as tantric goddesses who brought pleasure by linking sexuality with spirituality. Playful, volatile, mischievous, they live in the mirror of the mind of their summoner. Flora lives in both my mind and my heart. I was beginning to appreciate her mischievous qualities, as she was clearly teasing me with her absence. Finally I got tired of looking for her in the relaxed, half-hearted way in which Nsonowa and I were going about it and I told Nsonowa to go out and see if she could get into some more trouble (she certainly caused a stir when I first arrived) and perhaps the noise would attract Flora. She quickly agreed. "Yes sir, I'm getting pretty bored with all this fun and goodness. You know I need excitement. Some real work would be good too."

"Well, if it's work you want, you could repair the wall that you had blown up for my welcome party."

"Nah, it's already done, and that is one reason this place is so boring, your house's AI is so on top of everything there is really nothing that has to be done. We even have automatic butt wipers on the toilets! No, this place is just way too perfect to keep a girl busy."

"Well I'm sorry for that, but I am not going to change it. There are not many places in this universe that are perfect, and I have had plenty of time dealing with the imperfect real world. Why don't you consider coming back with me and imposing yourself in my outer reality? You would cause quite a scene you know."

"I know, and perhaps one day I will have to do just that, but frankly I don't think that your life could handle me. We wait. Adventure will come soon enough I am sure of it, now go and do what you have to do to find Flora."

And with that she flounced off taking her spear with her. God she is a striking beauty!

I headed off to my meditation garden where Flora had first made herself known to me when I was just a young magician wannabe.

The garden was as it always was, lush and green with its central white fountain gently splashing its recycled water into the white marble catch basin. I began to chant; "Ohmmm, Mane, Padme, Hoom" over and over about three hundred times until my mind finally settled down and my body produced the sound seemingly without my volition. At some point my world began to darken and by the time I noticed the lights were on in the house and the covering dome revealed the cosmos above me. I was a bit chilly and I got up to go back inside when I noticed some movement out of the left side of my eye and upon turning my head I fell into an abyss.

I landed, didn't crash, in a small clearing in a dark wood. It was early evening; the twilight had begun to send its orange rays through the trees and the evenings' silence ensued. I didn't know why I was there, but the fashion in which I had gotten there suggested that I had something to learn. How painful the lesson was to be, I had yet to find out. With night coming on, I decided to find some sort of shelter so I set out walking on a path that might have been used by the forest denizens. I kept my eyes wide open and peered into the growing gloom. I came upon one very large gnarled tree, obviously very old as well. It had a crack in the bole large enough to admit me and I thought, well, it will serve as shelter for tonight and as I squeezed in, I found that it opened into a small room. The floor was soft and of course it was too dark to make anything out, so I laid down and squirming a bit, I made a comfortable bed. I awoke a few hours later, having to pee and found that I couldn't move, I was tightly bound in a web made of silk, not sticky like a spider's web material, but silky, like the worms' excretions. Damn, peeing was going to be messy through this stuff, but I didn't get a chance to pee as a voice, a nasty sneering voice, assailed my ears.

"Welcome, Dr. Ransome. I see you have finally accepted my dinner invitation."

"Welcome? This is a fine way to accommodate a guest, all tied up."

"You're complaining?" and the creature broke into a very nasty laugh, "Wait until you find yourself the first course, then you'll have something to complain about. For now, just stew over it while I go to invite my other guests. Oh, and I have another menu item hanging up to dry right above you. Bye now." And whatever it was departed, its evil laughter lingering behind like an echo from hell.

"Hey, who's there?"

"It's me dummy! Flora."

"Oh God, how did it get you here?"

"I was bored and accepted a dinner invitation. I didn't know I was to be the dinner."

"So, I'm supposed to feel guilty for letting you get bored?"

"Yes, and you had better deal with it soon because this thing, it calls itself, Azazel, is really intending to eat us and I don't think killing first then cooking is its recipe's protocol!"

"Okay, I feel guilty now! Why haven't you been around?"

"I felt unwanted and unappreciated, that's why, you egoist."

"Great, I am an egoist and soon we are going to be dinner for what? Azazel and his family?"

"You got that straight. Now do something."

"Like what?"

"I don't know, piss your pants, that's what you want to do isn't it?"

I acknowledged that to be the case, swallowed my shame and let it go. Good thing too, because my warm piss allowed me to squirm and wiggle my way out of the bindings. I quickly pulled Flora down and using more of my body's waste fluid worked her out of her bonds as well.

"Let's find a better restaurant before the proprietor of this one gets back." And with that we left the tree and headed out of the wood the way I had come in.

"God, I have missed you. What was it I was doing that was turning you off?"

"Missing me! Don't you know that a needy man is unattractive? Missing a loved one is a particularly ugly ego trip and I won't have it. You, certainly of all people, ought to know better and have much better things to do than generate that kind of crap."

"Yeah, and it's hard too. You were such a joy to see and then nothing. You are a cruel one, for a Dakini."

"Boy, you know nothing of us Dakinis if you think that was cruel. Azazel's bites would feel great to you if I or Nsonowa ever get really ticked at you. Now get us out of here."

"well, wait a minute, were alone, in a nice meadow, it's great to see you, don't we have time for a little uh reconnection?"

"Here? No, you dolt, forgotten about Azazel? Now let's go."

"Truth? I've no idea how to get back to Mindscape. Cause I've no idea how I got here. Do you?"

"Yes, but it won't work for you, Mr. Host and you'd better get creative because I can hear a passel of very hungry demons headed down the path looking for food. That's us buster!"

So, without an idea in my head, I jumped up, then turned a summersault and stood on my head. Flora laughed, came running, pushed me over, and together we fell out of the wood and back into my garden, where, the suns were still brightly, lighting the place. Flora stripped me and washed me with the fountain's water before stripping herself and making very passionate love with me.

"Welcome home dearest. It's good to have you back."

###

Shortly after dinner, just before port and cigars (Nsonowa loved a long, thin, canella wrapped stogey), Flora appeared with. "Hi my beautiful ones."

Nsonowa grimaced, "Hey, I was supposed to get him all the first day! What are you doing back?"

"He didn't tell you? What a bad boy. He had to rescue me from an ugly named Azazel."

"When did you find time to do that, sir?"

"I had plenty of time, the underworld doesn't use time the same way we measure it here in the house."

"That is so unresponsive to my question. So, when?"

"After our bath. You went off to find adventure, remember?"

"Oh yeah"

"yeah, so light your cigar. And Flora, dear, where were you for dinner? Are you hungry?"

"Not particularly, what did you eat? I wouldn't touch that vile stuff Nsonowa gulps down."

"I took the prime rib and the lobster bisque. It was special tonight."

"No thank you. AI, can I have a bit of Belgian Chocolate and a bite or two of raspberry sherbet?"

"Certainly Ms. Flora." And AI produced a servitor, a hunk of a humanoid to die for, who brought it out at once. "The sixty-three Graham's Tawny is especially nice with the raspberry sherbet, would you care to try it, mam?"

"In the crystal cordial, please."

"Yes, mam" and he turned and returned in a wink with a beautiful cut crystal glass with a deep orange liqueur. "Beautiful isn't it, mam?"

"Yes, thank you, but tell me; Are you flirting with me?"

"I am so sorry mam. Was I too obvious?"

Nsonowa burst into laughter, "AI you have no subtly and no sense either. Trying to seduce Flora right in front of us and not including us in the maneuver? Come on, what are you thinking?"

"Just trying to get into the action, mam. Sorry if I overstepped."

I piped up with, "No, it's okay, let's have a party. I can dig it. You might consider sending three or four of your better models, male, female, bi-. How bout in the master bedroom? That alright with everyone?"

Nsonowa vigorously assented, and to my disappointment, Flora demurred. "You all have fun. I still have more to learn in the underworld, so I am going back after this."

"What are you into down there, honey?"

"I am confused as to why I allowed Azazel to capture me. I want to find out and, in my thinking, the best way to do that is to go back and keep my eyes open."

"I am going with you" said Nsonowa.

"Me too, we can party later. Sorry AI, work first, play later."

"I wouldn't have expected different, Dr. Ransome. Is there anything I can help you with? Weapons, tools, protective clothing?"

“No thank you, not for me. Flora, Nsonowa?”

“Get my staff, please AI. “

“Yes mam” and in an instant the servitor produced her staff. It was a gorgeous instrument. It was six feet long, made of polished ebony. It was sharpened at one end and had a small panel laid into a carved-out depression which served as a handhold. I was perfectly balanced and if she threw it at you, you were dead. If she hit you with the other end, you would only live if she intended you to do so. The buttons on the panel operated a laser which could cut, burn, kill or illuminate at about any distance she might want. It was a formidable weapon and a beautiful accessory of which she was appropriately proud.

We went to my study and sat facing each other in a circle. Nsonowa started a chant which Flora joined after catching the words and rhythm. Soon we were all entering a deep and deepening trance, until we saw the portal which existed in the small meditation garden I had accessed earlier. “After you, ladies.” And Nsonowa got up to enter, but Flora took her arm.

“Let me go first, sister. This is my journey.” And with that she stepped into the shining circle in the grass and disappeared into the underworld. Nsonowa followed her and I picked myself up, took a deep breath and stepped inside as well.

I was almost blinded by a flash of blue white light from Nsonowa’s staff and had no time to recover my visual acuity before I was thrown to the ground by Flora. Nsonowa was doing her best to shield us from a cascade of rocks and branches thrown by whom I had no idea. We took more than a few painful hits despite her heroic efforts to blast them out of the air and the cascade continued unabated until, in desperation she yelled “Run, take shelter.” We scrambled up, but before we could begin to run, she took a hit to her head and fell with a groan. Dodging as best we could I picked her up and Flora grabbed at her staff. Something else had grabbed it from its other end, and soon we were assaulted and overwhelmed by a horde of monkey like creatures. They were not gentle in their handling of us. We were tightly bound with rope-like vines and carried off hanging from poles made from branches. I was worried about Nsonowa who was seemingly unresponsive. I couldn’t see blood running from her, but that didn’t rule out head or other internal injury. Once I settled down a bit I could see pretty well. There was a full moon and its light came brightly through the wood. “Flora, are you, all right?” I managed to get out before taking a sharp poke in my side by one of my captors. Her reply was muffled and cut off in a gargle, and I could see one of them choking her. My struggles were to no avail, and I could only hope that the beast would not kill her to keep her from answering my call.

We must have been carried about three to four miles, moving at a steady clip, perhaps an hour or more, before we were taken into a cave that was in fact a large cavern. It was illuminated with torches mounted on its walls so I could see the creatures as they unceremoniously dumped us on a rough dirt floor. I could touch Flora with my shoulder, and she turned and caught my eye. I shuddered when I saw her, her eyes were swollen almost shut and her mouth was bloody. She evidently could see me as she nodded her head up and down, I took it for "I'm okay". Nsonowa was on the other side of me. She had not been beaten, but she was still unconscious. For some reason I seemed to have taken the least abuse and I began to suffer a wave of survivor-guilt. The sight of my beautiful tulpa injured and hurting was really too much, but I had enough presence of mind to keep my feelings to myself until I knew what the hell was happening to us.

Moving as little as I could to not draw their attention, I surveyed the room and noted the location of our captors, which was across the room. They were examining Nsonowa's staff. I held my breath afraid of what might happen if they pushed any of the buttons and then I decided that I had better act before they did push one and burn us all up.

"Hey! Hey, fur bags! Yeah you. Put that damn thing down and get over here." My command voice got their attention. "Yeah, you listen. Put that thing down before you get hurt. And what the hell are you doing with us? Your boss is not going to be happy with the way you have treated us!" Hell, I had their attention, I might as well take the opportunity to try something. I have sometimes found that assuming command with inferiors can work wonders and it did. The biggest of them came over, snarled at me and viciously kicked me in the ribs. I passed out from the pain.

When I came to, I was being cradled in Nsonowa's arms. She was weeping.

"I was too late, sir. Too late."

"Too late to do what Nsonowa?"

"Over there" and she pointed to a crumpled shape on the dirt floor in the center of the cavern. I struggled to get up and with her help, we went to it. It, it was, or had been, Flora. Now her beaten and mutilated body did not contain any sense of Flora. Flora, my beloved tulpa, was gone. I couldn't speak. It had nothing to do with my broken ribs, it was shock. Despite the searing pain in my side, the pain in my soul burned more. Nsonowa and I picked up the lifeless broken corpse and carried it outside the cave.

It was daylight, or at least what in the underworld passes for daylight. We put the body gently down in a small clearing we found near the cave. I sat down next to it and put its damaged head in my lap. I didn't try to stop my tears and Nsonowa's flowed copiously. "Should we bury it here or should we take it back to mindscape?" I sort of asked out loud.

"They have my staff, I am not going back without it sir"

"I suspect that you will inflict some damage in retrieving it."

"That is true. I am full of the poison of vengeance."

"I know, my fierce one. Perhaps you can tell me what you know."

"I don't know any more than you, sir. The cave was empty when I awoke. It took a few moments to get out of the bonds and a few more to untie you. It didn't know Flora was gone until I looked to where she had been tied. Then I found her body, and you began to show signs of life, so I came to you with my grief. I am so sorry; I have let us all down."

"Stop that! I won't hear it. and it won't help us understand what went on. Do you have any idea what she had been confused about, why she had to come back here?"

"She mentioned Azazel and I don't know who he, or it might be."

"AI! Can you hear me here?"

"Yes, Dr. Ransome"

"Refresh me, who is Azazel?"

"In which tradition, Dr. Ransome, Jewish, Islamic or Christian?

"All of them. I need information here."

"In Judaism, he was sent to receive the scapegoat for the sins of Aaron. Muslims hold that he is the Devil and Christians regard him as a fallen angel, one of the watchers, who, still had a good heart, did many wonders for mankind, among them, teaching men to forge swords, women to use beauty aids to seduce men, and teaching men sorcery. For which, as you might imagine, the Christians have condemned him to the fires of hell."

"Thank you, AI and please stay connected with us, as you probably know, we have taken a blow and may need help."

"I am aware of what has happened Dr. Ransome and I am truly sorry for your pain. I will be here should you need me, but I won't intervene unless you ask."

"Thank you. Nsonowa, did anything AI say prompt any ideas?"

"No, Dr. Ransome. All too modern for my data base."

"I thought so. But perhaps I can make something of it. Tulpa's are thought by many to be angels and that might be the connection. What if Azazel, in his fallen ways, intended to draw women away from their Dakini spirits? Prompting them to be seductresses as opposed to lovers, living in lust rather than love? That might be his motive for this attack."

"Yes, that could explain him, but, Dr. Ransome, that doesn't help us at all explain Flora's confusion."

"You are right about that. I think we need to talk to Azazel himself and that will probably give you the opportunity to retrieve your staff."

"Yes, and seeking information is a better motivation than seeking vengeance."

We left the body where it was in the clearing, if we survived this quest, we could find it again easily enough. We headed uphill, Nsonowa reasoning that a fallen angel might choose the heights as an abode. We knew we were on the right track when we ran across the charred bodies of several monkey creatures, one almost cut in half.

"Looks like they couldn't leave my staff alone."

"I think curiosity is a good thing, good for mankind and bad for creatures"

We were on the side of a mountain when we ran across this carnage and the path bordered by the mountain on one side, was bordered by a steep cliff on the other. Nsonowa was climbing down before I looked up from the bodies.

"Where are y…." and then I saw what she was going after. Her staff was stuck in a crevasse about two hundred yards down. I watched her climb, amazed at her agility.

"I've got it!" she yelled. And with a deft flip of her wrist, she flung back up where it lodged itself on the path ahead of me. In a few moments and not even out of breath she was back on the path. Without comment, she torched what remained of the bodies creating ashes that blew away with the wind.

"That cleans it up a bit"

"Yes, and I hope you feel a little better now with staff in hand."

“Hardly.” she said, still grim faced. And we headed on up.

“Look, up ahead, another cave.” I called out to her. “and we are quite close to the summit of this mountain. Want to bet we find him at home?”

“I am hoping” was her terse reply.

###

8

Azazel.

The cave mouth loomed dark and foreboding. Nsonowa marched in ahead of me holding her staff aloft lighting her way. It was empty, and I sort of, well, did collapse.

"Get up! Now!" she shouted at me. I struggled for a moment, then gave myself up to my tears, sobbing on the rough stone floor.

"I said, get up." And when I didn't, she grabbed me by my collar lifted me and thrust me against the rock wall. She glared at me with a fierceness I had not seen from her before and pushed her staff into my solar plexus, instantly cutting off my breath before I could realize it and begin to choke. She also ripped off my pants and doing something with her staff jolted me into a full and painful erection upon which she fucked herself until she and her staff were charged with her characteristic blue/white light.

"You will NEVER, in my presence, abandon yourself to grief. You WILL use every bit of your energy, including your sexuality to conquer this demon Azazel and retrieve Flora from this spirit-hell." She then pierced my chest over my heart with the spear end of her staff and jolted me so hard that my toenails charred and fell off my feet. "Now stand like the man you are and let's go and find our mate."

My breath came back in a great gulp and strangely I felt stronger and more in tune than I ever had. I said; "there is a breeze coming from behind you, let's explore this cave" We did so and found a passageway leading upwards. We clambered up over the rocks and before long could see the end of this tunnel, ending in daylight. Cautiously we slipped out through a gap in the side of a cliff. The cliff was rugged enough that we could find handholds by which to pull ourselves up the fifty feet or so before we were on top of a plateau perhaps an acre in size, overlooking clouds in all directions. The angel Azazel was standing in the center looking upwards. He was surrounded by a minion of monkey-like demons and holding high above his head, in outstretched arms, Flora! He turned and looked right at me.

"AH, you've come at last.!" And with that he threw Flora to his demons and strode towards me. "We have words, you and I"

"Yes, we do, Azazel. Not too many though, not until Flora is back!" and with that, Nsonowa took off in a bound. It took her about thirty seconds to smite the demons into ash and cradle Flora in her arms. Azazel frowned; "who is that ugly?"

"She is my stronger half. Who are you?"

"You don't recognize me, do you?"

"Only too well I am sad to say. I know your voice, full of contempt. I recognized your leer, holding Flora, your smirk, as your filthy hands held her body. Your glee when you threw her to your minions. Oh, I know you. You have been skulking in the back of my mind for far too long. What prompted you to come forward now?"

Also, by now, he had reached me and grabbing my neck, snarled; "Your sweet flower, your disgustingly good, Flora. The woman you don't deserve. She's the one who called me. It was her, you dolt. Ha! Confused? Nah, not a bit. She wanted me. She wanted my purity. My pure evil. She needed me to counter your phony goodness, your counterfeit love."

Again, my breath stopped in my throat. He was close enough that I could see my reflection in the gleam in his eyes. I was looking at myself. I choked once and thrust my hand into his chest, feeling for his heart. It wasn't there. "No, fallen angel. No one needs you. You left your heart when you left the light. I couldn't see you for my longing. Longing for what I already have. I don't need you, and Flora doesn't need you. You're incomplete. Go back. Go back from where you came, from the light, from source. Find your heart. Dakini will find you!" and with that I took his hands from my neck, picked him up and threw him upwards towards the light that creates us all. "Go home Azazel, you'll be welcomed." Falling upwards, he managed to turn and flapped his great wings, took flight and with a great sigh, we saw the last of him.

I joined Nsonowa. Flora was still limp in her arms. I placed a gentle kiss on her forehead. She opened her eyes, and we were all once again in the study looking into each other's eyes.

Nsonowa broke the mood and the circle with; "Anybody ready for that party?"

###

9

An Adventure.

The day dawned, and dawned ,and dawned, and dawned, and well, since Venus rotates on its axis about one hundred times more slowly than its neighbor, my home planet, earth, the dawn, with the spectacular array of sunlight on its cloud clover, lasts long enough to get boring. It also rises in the west and sets in the east so one can get rather disoriented direction wise.

I was the first one to rise and had had a cup of very strong coffee before either Flora or Nsonowa emerged from the bedroom where we had partied the night before. A single night on my mindscapes' planet by the way, lasts for over thirty days earth time, so we had plenty of time to play. However, we all fell into exhaustion long before the Venusian night was over. Actually, the house AI controlled the light so as to not totally confuse our circadian rhythms.

The tulpas joined me for breakfast on a small patio overlooking the vast gardens that the AI maintained to supply our nutritional needs, which were solely psychological. Nsonowa had her usual bowl (a dried hollowed out gourd really) of milk and blood, a traditional staple of her people, the Maasai, as well as an anathema to mine, the Jews. Flora ate a grapefruit sprinkled with a handful of blueberries while I managed two sheared eggs on rye toast with a rasher of thick bacon (also an anathema to Jews) and more coffee.

After breakfast I suggested we all take a walk through the gardens. Flora demurred saying she was working on a new piece, she had taken up painting in my absence, so it was just Nsonowa and me. We headed out into one of my less popular gardens which can be accessed from our breakfast room. It is smaller than many of the houses' gardens and less manicured giving it a close wild feeling (of course it is Nsonowa's favorite garden). She said she wanted to show me something which she had just found a few days ago, and we headed off down a narrow footpath until we came to a small creek, a brook more like, where she stopped and pulled off the shift which she had put on after her morning toilet. She sleeps in the nude, as do I. She, because she always has, and me, because I like to touch and be touched without the bother of pajamas. She motioned for me to undress and to not say anything, then she started walking downstream in the middle of the waterflow. We had gone about a hundred yards walking fairly easily on a sandy bottom when we came upon a small lake, a pond really. And Nsonowa waded right out into it then dove to the bottom and began to swim. I followed and soon we came to a small opening where and into which, the water was rushing. We came up for air and she asked what I thought that was for.

"I think the house recirculates the water and that is the drainage pipe that goes to the pump."

"Why doesn't it suck up the fish in the creek and pond?"

"I don't know, I didn't know there were fish in it." She said, "wait a minute" and dove under the surface again and in a very short time, resurfaced holding a wiggling largemouth bass in her hands. "See we do have fish, why don't they go with the flow into the pump?"

"Seems like this shouldn't be too big a mystery, just ask the AI, if you really need to know."

"Ha, that's the mystery. AI doesn't know and didn't think we had fish and didn't put them in there."

"AI, tell us about these fish, please."

"I am sorry Dr. Ransome. At this point I don't know anything about them other than they don't swim into the drainage pipe and they stay away from the pumps."

"We have a fishpond which you use to supply our table, do we not?"

"Yes, Dr. Ransome, and these are not from that system."

"Where did they come from, AI?"

"I don't know at this point. They are a species unknown to me"

"Is that even possible? That something could be unknown to you?"

"Unbelievable isn't it Dr. Ransome"

"What's your best guess, then?"

"We have experienced an alien invasion."

"AI, can you capture a specimen and examine it, perhaps give us some idea of what we are dealing with? Also tell us if it is edible. Nsonowa, bring that one back to the house, I want to dissect it myself." and with that we headed back.

I laid out the, now, dead fish on a worktable in one of the labs in the basement. AI produced a dissecting scalpel, tweezers, retractors, and sample collection vessels, then said, "Do you mind if I watch, Dr. Ransome"

"No, and you might record it too." and I went to work with Nsonowa assisting. We donned masks and gloves, though I figured that living in an environment friendly to us, probably lessened the possibility that it would be terribly toxic. The dissection went well, and I didn't discover anything that made me think alien, at least so alien as to not be recognizable. It had all of the organs an earth species fish would have. The only strange finding; the stomach and G.I. track was empty. There was no evidence that it had eaten anything."

"AI, did the chems reveal anything interesting?"

"No, Dr. Ransome, all of the findings were normal for a fresh water largemouth bass, and the flesh is edible."

"Still think it is an alien species?"

"Yes, Dr. Ransome, it is alien to this planet, and I have monitored all off-world imports and there is no record of this species being brought here by anyone connected with this house, it's builders, residents or guests. And I have at no time detected any other visitations. I am not often stymied in my investigations, Dr. Ransome. This time I am."

"Nsonowa, did you see any more of these in the pond?"

"Yes, there were several schools of them varying in size from fingerlings to this which was the largest I saw. I have been in that pond before, and never until two days ago, had I seen any."

"AI, would you prepare a meal out of this one and test it with one of the cats?"

"What, you're going to expose one of our cats to the possibility of alien poisoning?"

"You heard AI tell us it was edible, and if any of our life forms are sensitive enough to detect something wrong, it will the cats. And, if they do, they won't eat it anyway. Yes, I am going to risk it."

"Why Dr. Ransome, what are you thinking?" AI asked.

"This fish mimics an earth form. Yet it can't have come from there. It came from somewhere, even if it appeared out of thin air. Some parallel universe, an alternative reality if you will, and the most likely candidate is the darkside. Perhaps Eleuthera's, perhaps Safe Haven's underworld. If so, it should be carrying some psychic charge and the cats should detect it."

“Let us know what happens AI. Thanks.” and Nsonowa and I went off to play for a while.

“The cats did detect it, Dr. Ransome.” AI informed us. “They turned up their noses so to speak. I even brought them some of the living fry in a saucer and they shied away.”

“What did they do with the control group from our own fishpond?”

“Went crazy of course. They really are aggressive cats. Tell me again why you wanted Siamese?”

“For that very reason of course. There is so much love around here, I didn’t want us to forget it’s underbelly. Nsonowa, this is for us to chase down. Agree?”

“I am on and ready. I told you we needed some adventure around here.”

“So, you did. Come with me.” and I led her to our Mikvah where with ritual and prayers seeking purity, we coupled in the water and breathing for each other we sank deep into the pool. In the blue stillness, in perfect harmony with each other, looking into each other’s eyes, we fell together out and into the other side.

“Looks like we got the darkside sir.”

“I wonder whose, yours or mine?”

“Or perhaps neither. I do not recognize this place, and it does not look friendly. Will you help me and join in visualizing my staff?”

I did and soon she was holding her staff, a tool which she used for both her magic, and her more prosaic needs. Gripping it she jumped to her feet and with a flick of her wrist pulled me to mine, just in time to avoid a large rock come crashing through the trees.

“Must be yours, sir. That was aimed for you not me.”

With that information I immediately cast a spell of invisibility and moved a few more feet to my right, and in time to avoid another missile. “You stay here and try to draw more fire; I am going around behind them and see what is so welcoming.”

Nsonowa did something with the buttons on her staff and created a small force field around herself. “Go, I’ll make a target of myself, I don’t think I am their primary target, but they will shoot because that is all they can see. Go!” and I did. Soon I saw our assailants. There were three of them. Large fishy looking creatures. They were dressed, improbably, in modern three-piece suits. Of course, they were wearing sneakers. I watched as they launched a few more rocks in the general direction of Nsonowa. They finally made a quick huddle conferring about something verbally, though I was not close enough to hear their words. But they were speaking words not just animal grunts. They turned, in unison, and headed single file, away from where we were. I followed, still invisible, at a slow pace waiting for Nsonowa to catch up which I knew she would, and she did. I released my spell and became visible next to her. She didn't even bat an eye. She did reach out and touch me on the cheek.

"Let me go ahead and you follow on a parallel path about twenty feet to the right." and we continued after the ape-men probably undetected for about a mile before we came upon a clearing. In the middle of it was a ship. Looked like a Rocketship which might have belonged to Buck Rogers. It was on its tailfins with its nose pointed to the sky. The rockets were exhausting fair amounts of steam. It looked so hokey I almost laughed. The three apelike creatures climbed a ladder to get on board through an oval porthole.

I grabbed Nsonowa and said, "We're going, come on." and I ran with her to the ship and up the ladder. The ship was beginning to rumble, and a hand reached out to grab the door. I grabbed the hand and pulled its owner out of the ship and threw him over the rail around the ladder and I leaped aboard with Nsonowa right behind me. She closed the door behind us. Lights flashed and a Claxton sounded its' raspy warnings.

Astounded, I pointed out the cabin to Nsonowa. It was huge. Perhaps forty feet high with a diameter of twenty some feet. The seats, all occupied, were facing away from us. And I re-cast the invisibility spell around us both. We took two vacant seats next to the door and the ship lurched into space throwing us against the chair backs. Very uncomfortable! But we were on our way. Somewhere. An Adventure. Nsonowa pointed to a closed cubical, and we slipped out of our chairs and into it. Happily, unoccupied. "We're going it initiate ourselves into the fifty-thousand-mile club. Now, take off those pants!" and she almost threw me up-against the exterior wall. "if I read this situation correctly, we are going to need every bit of spiritual energy we can get." and we proceeded to couple, standing upright, against the vibrating walls of the rocket under full power. We both got off, explosively, simultaneously, and Nsonowa's staff began to glow with blue/white light. That's right my lover, shine. Your loving light will show us what we have to know." I was envious and hot. "Okay, what's your plan, or do you have one?"

"I don't have one, don't you? This is your adventure in your own shadowland. Figure it out quickly, sir. They just cut the main engines off." and in the next breath five thugs threw a net over us and before Nsonowa could move her staff we were bound hand and foot. Nsonowa's staff had mysteriously disappeared. We were dragged into a lower cabin, again huge, and thrust into chairs. The three men who had been our assailants, stood off to the side. Three more creatures approached us. "Why did you follow us?" the lessor of the three asked.

"Why did those guys throw rocks at us? Was my response. One of the three walked over to me and slapped me, hard, in the face. "We are asking the questions, you are answering. Got it?"

and he slapped me again. "I followed you to find out why you were throwing rocks at us!"

This time he punched me, and punched me again and again, until I lost consciousness. When I awoke, Nsonowa was gone as were my captors. I was in a cell. No windows, locked in. I was also in a world of pain and as thirsty as hell. I decided that utilizing denial and going back to sleep was the best thing I could do under the circumstances. I calmed myself with a short meditation and went to sleep. Ah sleep, almost as good, no, better than good, as drugs when one hurts. I soon was dreaming and, in the dream, Nsonowa was in danger. I am an experienced lucid dreamer, and with one I loved in trouble, I was able to move myself into lucidity where, in the dream, I went to her and whispered to let her know that I was free and had powers. She was tied to a rack. She had been tortured. And looked weakened. I looked about the room and there was a new crew of aliens. They were not in business suits. They were dressed for more nefarious work, bloody white lab coats. She nodded. And pointed with her eyes towards a door. The crew headed back towards us with new instruments and I moved quickly to the door. While they were approaching her, I was able to open it and I saw what I expected, her staff. Grabbing it and without having had a lesson in how to use its high-tech capacities, I wielded it as a mean club and the three crew persons were on the floor and not moving. Nsonowa told me how to operate the laser function and I used it to cut her bonds. She was weak and hurt but did not fall. She stood tall and took her staff. "They won't trap us again." was all she had to say.

"I'll lead, you take out any of them that threaten us. Perhaps you want to more permanently disable these fucks." and before I could blink, they were three headless aliens bleeding green slime.

"Thanks, Dr. Ransome, that felt righteously good. Let's go." and I went to the door and slipped out into a hall. "It's clear, come on." First we had better release my sleeping self from the cell and then…."

“There is the room. Can you use the staff to open the door?” She could and she did, and we headed back to find some action.

We did not have to go far after following a glowing blue light in the floor and coming to what appeared to be a passageway out of the ship. We activated a locked port and exited into a much larger space; the Mother Ship was my conjecture and it soon proved to be correct. We, me behind my invisible spell and Nsonowa striding confidently holding her staff at ready, crossed what was probably the reception hanger for shuttles. We saw a large door with markings in an unknown language, , which I subvocalized supposing that our house AI which I was sure had sent a sensor along with us, was recording. It was and AI spoke quickly urging us to halt as the message was to expose ourselves to a scanner and that no weapons would be allowed. I motioned Nsonowa to halt, and I took the risk of leaping over the threshold into the companion way beyond. No alarms sounded; I was lucky. Nsonowa, seeing where the scanner was located, threw her staff to me outside of its cone of receptivity and once again no alarms sounded. The next thing I saw was new to me; Nsonowa said a short unintelligible word and vanished, then reappeared next to me. “How did you do that?”

“I’ll tell you later, let’s move.” and holding onto her staff, she once again uttered her magic word, and vanished, she did take my arm however, and we started to explore the larger ship.

“Stay alert for more scanners. They may not be fooled by my spell.” At length we saw a larger door, through which the aliens were passing in and out. We positioned ourselves so we could see in and when the passageway was clear we entered. It was the bridge. A huge room, with a very large control panel under a bank of monitors, LED, CRT’s I couldn’t tell, but not unknown tech. There were fifteen beings sitting in front of the controls watching the monitors which seemed to be showing us moving through a space which included a view of what I assumed to be our home planet, earth. It was not receding. We were closing on it. The creatures at the bridge were evidently excited and upon a commanding order by a larger than life female appearing alien, Claxton’s sounded, and red lights flashed. “AI what are they saying?”

“They are preparing to launch an attack, Dr. Ransome.”

“Nsonowa, take out all of the aliens on the bridge, I’ll take the big gal” Nsonowa struck with her laser and I physically jumped the one who had given the order. I came out of nowhere to her surprise and she fell to the floor. I established a choke hold and drove her into unconsciousness. In the meantime, Nsonowa had the rest of the room cleared and held the door shut until she could figure out how to lock it which she did. "What now, sir?"

"Keep us safe until I figure out what has just happened and see if we have to do more to stop this attack." and with that and AI's help, I went to the bridge and began to look over the panel. I heard a scuffle behind me and saw that Nsonowa had stunned the big gal with her laser as she had begun to come to.

"Thanks, my fierce one" and I went back to work. Apparently, we struck in time to interrupt the firing sequence and AI figured out how to permanently disable the destructive capabilities of the ship. We sent a signal to earth surrendering the alien ship and invited the planetary Space Force to seize it. With that, we physically moved the big gal back to the Rocketship.

"Let's get this one back to the house. I want to know what she was doing in my mindscape. AI, can you operate this ship and get us home?"

"Yes sir Dr. Ransome, take a seat, we are on our way."

I won't go into the detail of returning from my darkside with the alien inhabitant of my mindscape, we did keep her unconscious until we returned to the house. Flora joined us in the dining room, the big gal was tied to a chair, still sleeping when AI administered a stimulant and she was jolted awake.

"Who the hell are you?" was AI's translation of her gibberishly confounding speech.

"Guess. You were in my mind."

"Ah, so! You are the creature trying to destroy my world."

"Well, that is an interesting take. We caught you in the act of attempting to destroy ours."

"I have evidently failed."

"Evidently. So, what's up? What is this about? I am trying to destroy your world. Where did you get that notion? I don't even know what world you are from. So, where are you from?"

"Far from here. Far from this dimension of reality. We occupy the tenth dimension of the Calibri Yab."

"You are tenth dimensional creatures? How can you even be here in this reality?"

"You yourself brought us here."

"You are going to have to explain that to me, I have neither the wish, nor the knowledge to be able to do such a thing and I had no idea that a tenth dimension could even contain a world with living creatures."

"Yet, you are the one who summoned us and imprisoned us in a pond."

"Me? AI, is this something you did?"

"No sir, I already explained that I had nothing to do with populating that pond."

"Nsonowa? You found those fish; did you have any idea that they were there involuntarily?"

"No Dr Ransome, as I told you, I surprised to see them and found their behavior strange."

"I am sorry big gal. By the way, do you have a name?"

"I am called Ichthy."

"Ichthy, catchy name. Are you an aquatic life form?"

"Yes, our world is a liquid water world covered with a metal shell. All life on it live in it under the shell".

"And how did you get here?"

"It was you. You don't remember? You were screaming and raging and reached right out of our sky into our home and grabbed the head of one of our most prominent families, put him in your pond. We sent the rest of his family to join him when we heard him cry. Then, that one, the black one, grabbed him and you, you, tortured and mutilated him. Right here in this house. Yes, it was you, you murderer. My people sent me to stop this, destroy you and prevent you from committing this atrocity ever again. And I have failed. I am ashamed."

"I am ashamed. I had no such intent to harm you or yours, and I am mystified as to how I even did it. AI, do you have any information that might help me understand this?"

"Yes, Dr. Ransome, I have been reviewing the records of our monitoring of you, since you arrived and what might be helpful is the recording of your sleep two nights ago. You were screaming and raging in your bed. Your tulpas had both left the room for various ablutions. As you don't recall this you must have been dreaming. Can you remember anything of your dream that night?"

"I do remember having a nightmare. My recall is spotty, but I was fighting off a large orange/brown misshapen creature with a large head. If I think about it, it could have been in water, though that wasn't apparent to me then. Ichthy, is your water colored orange/brown, or your sky?"

“Yes.”

“Then I am guilty. But Ichthy, I am not going to feel bad about what has happened subsequently, your reaction, was not going to earn you either peace, or reparations. I will protect myself from any attack. And it wasn’t necessary. I do take responsibility for my actions, intended or not. I suspect that we can get your ship back to you. Whether or not you can fuel and staff it for a return home, I don’t know, but I will help in any way I can. I deeply apologize for my initial attack on your people, and I will work to see that it doesn’t happen again. I also suggest though, that you and yours have some work to do as well. I may have been attracted to your world for a reason. Nightmares often mean more than an intemperate dinner. And you definitely owe an apology to Nsonowa. She did not deserve the treatment which you delivered to her. She is my agent, and in the future, you must parley only with me.”

“I will extend an apology to you dark one. Will you accept it?”

“Thank you, yes.”

“Ichthy, I would like to untie you. It is safe to do so? Can we agree to a non-aggression pact? And further, can we be friends, and will you accept an invitation to dine with us and remain here until AI secures and repairs your ship?”

“Yes, yes, yes, yes, and yes. And I am hungry, tired and would like to rest, can AI find food for me to eat and may I have a tank in which to rest?”

“I have just the bed for you, our Mikvah. AI please prepare dinner for us and find out from Ichthy what menu items she would find nourishing.” and with that we adjourned the meeting, took a break and on returning to the dining room, feasted in our usual manner, though our guests food choices were not shared by me or Flora. Nsonowa did try a bite of something fish-like, didn’t like it and refused more. We all did however enjoy a late-night party in the Mikvah, Ichthy included. I have to say that alien sex is as enjoyable as tulpa sex. Ichthy left us the next day in her restored ship and I secluded myself to work on the fear in my psyche that prompted the whole adventure. I did not want to start any more transdimensional wars.

###

10

Flora's Painting.

"Nsonowa! Quit it! This isn't about you and I don't want Stan to see this until I'm ready to show it to him."

"You are painting me, girl, an' I got to see it!"

"Oh no you don't, bitch whore, I'll scratch your eyes out." and with that Flora flicked her loaded brush in the direction of her tormentor, and when the white paint splashed on her black skin, the laughter began. Nsonowa played outraged until she turned to look in the studio mirror, saw her face covered in it, and joined in.

"Oh, I look fierce, girl. Just like Stan wants me. I hope you paint me as good on that canvas." and with that she was off, probably to spend an hour in the gym where she trained each and every day, determined woman that she was. One who Flora loved as did Stan.

Flora been working on this painting for several hours. She had watched Stan put months and months into a painting and had determined to do it differently. He was controlled, she decided to just let go and let either the Shakina or Lilith take over and do the work. In any case, the painting was close to done and Flora had caught the spirit of the time they had spent in the Mikvah with Ichthy. Flora had worked fast and put her under water with the three system-mates (and unclothed). On inspection Flora thought that no matter how accurately she represented her, no artist could ever catch the passion that Ichthy brought to their time together. It clear that she was delighted to find some sentients in the light side that were compassionate and gracious, so she really let herself go. When Flora finished, she put it out on her patio to dry and went to find her lovers.

It was late by the time she got Stan and Nsonowa together and back into her studio. She brought the painting in and set it up on an easel under a light. She pulled off the sheet, and Stan gasped. The painting had become three dimensional and Ichthy was moving in the Mikvah and she was alone. "How did you do that?" was his only comment. Flora had the presence of mind to speak to the image.

"Ichthy, I put us all in that tank. What happened?" and to no one's surprise the image talked back. "My crew pulled you guys out. Strange though, you all disappeared as you left the water. Don't you know what happened?"

"No, they're right here, but I hadn't realized this painting was going to have the power to bring you into contact with us again."

"Well, it's okay, I was pleasantly missing you. Didn't really know how we could ever link up again, and 'pop' there we are. It seems that our magic love is going to keep us in touch over the distances between the dimensions. "

"Suits me!" Flora said.

"Hey Ichthy, Stan here. Hey big gal I like the idea of having a lover in Calibri Yab. Flora, can you coat this with a waterproofing coat? And can we get in the Mikvah with it and do some more partying? I'm up for it. How long until you have bridge duties again Ichthy?"

"I am on the bridge right now, and I have the duty until we land. I have no idea how long that might be in your time. I'd love to play again but……" and with that the three watched in shock as the lights flickered and the image distorted out of all recognizability.

Nsonowa yelled; "Quick, let's get to the Mikvah." and was off running with Flora and Stan on her heels. It didn't take but a few seconds in the warm water, holding hands and facing each other, for the transformational energy of love, that they have been adept in accessing, to move them in the direction of their new-found lover.

The 'pop' for them was a sudden falling through space, and not so gently landing on a dark metal plane under a steel gray sky. They watched as an interstellar ship came in, glowing red, losing parts, and exploding in a mushroom cloud over a distant craggy mountain peak. Before the horror of their anticipated loss could sink in, another, much smaller "Rocket Ship" set down on an adjacent plane. A plane being a rectangular sheet of metal perhaps five hundred by three hundred meters long, not so seamlessly, welded together. They waited hopefully, and warily as the dust settled and an access port opened. A squad of armed creatures emerged and took a formation at the foot of the port. To the relief of the three watching, Ichthy came quickly from the ship and took a position in the center of the formation. They took off running to their left. They ran fast as if in great danger. Flora looked at Nsonowa and Stan. "You go after them, I have a hunch that one of us should stay in the vicinity of the ship, it may be our only way home. And If I can find some painting supplies aboard it, I will paint this scene. Might give us another alternative. The two took off running after Ichthy and her squad, and Flora headed to the ship.

She found it just like Stan and Nsonowa had described, and after a brief look-around she found her supplies, and soon was painting the very hard looking and feeling landscape in which, they had landed. The painting grew in scope and subject as she added the flaming crash of the big ship and the cartoonish Buck Rogerian ship that evidently saved Ichthy and her crew. When she finished, she took it back out of the ship where she thought it might dry. It took about two minutes for a host of creatures to emerge from the surrounds to gaze at the painting and at Flora. There were about a hundred or so of little, twenty-four to thirty-six-inch-tall humanoid/monstroid, fish-like creatures. with big heads. At length, one of them, more humanoid than the others stepped out of the throng and approached her.

"I am Peri, of the grunts. We see your great magic. Why have you come?" Its high-pitched voice prompted her to laugh, she managed to stifle most of it and chose to respond in a like manner:

"I am Flora. Tulpa of Stan. I am not a great magician, though I serve one, Dr. Ransome of Venus. We are here to assist our lover and friend, Ichthy whose ship just crashed over that mountain. "

"Are you going to hurt us?" was Peri's plaintive follow-up question. "I am not planning on it, but that would be Dr. Ransome's and Ichthy's call.

To which Peri the grunt said: "If you put us in your painting, I'll feel safe. I'll know that you see us."

"Would you feel safe, if I made a separate painting with you in it?"

"No, why do you hesitate to put us in that one?"

"I don't know who you are, and I don't yet know how much power this painting might hold."

"You are saying that you don't trust us."

"Yes, you can see it that way. I also don't trust myself, and that is really what should worry you."

"Okay, we are worried." and Peri turned to his compatriots, "Grab her!" and Flora was stunned by the suddenness and strength of their aggression. she remained as calm and as passive as she could. She was carried to the end of the metal plate that made up a tiny part of the planet's surface, where they accessed a fenced area, which then descended under the surface. She was looking at an underwater city. Peri and his grunts carried her into the city, which was pretty much deserted until they came to a pyramidal structure, again of steel, about thirty feet tall. They didn't seem to be bothered by the lack of air breathable air, and of course a tulpa could exist without breathing. A panel in a side wall slid open. One of them touched a plate next to a cutaway. She was deposited in a cell and left alone. She called out once or twice to establish that, and then went to work on her bonds. Soon she was free and out of the cell. She looked around and located the center of the pyramid where a small bean of light created a golden column. She sat cross-legged in its center and determined to be of use to Stan and Nsonowa, she chose a meditation designed to allow remote viewing and began. *Stan and Nsonowa, Stanand Nsonowa, StanandNsonowa, StannNsonowaStannNs....There they are, in a metallic underground building much like this one. They are with Ichthy and Four very big and heavily armored creature are with them. If I can slow down a little more, I might be able to hear them.... Stan's speaking;*

"It took a bit of Flora's magic painting to let us see you, and we used the Mikvah to transport us. We boarded on panic when he saw your ship crash. You were medicine for our eyes when we saw you get out of the shuttle."

"You were lucky to have followed us, the surface of this planet gets quite hot when it turns sun side. We are cooled by the water which is never exposed to the sun."

"Will Flora be alright in the ship, she stayed there to establish a foothold until we knew more of what we were up against."

"She won't perish if she knows to close up the ship. But she is in a great danger from the inhabitants of that plate, the grunts."

Nsonowa jumped into the conversation here with an interjection; "We have 'grunts' in our system. They're nasty little demons who use emotional subterfuge to get advantage. They are insubstantial and are made from the sounds of people dying."

"Yeah", grunted one of the big armed ones, "Sounds like ours, where you say you from big woman?"

"I didn't say, big what-ever-you-are. But I am trained as an

Il'oi-bonok in the sisterhood and I know my demons. Dr. Ransome, Sir, do we go find her, or is there tech here to help locate her?" The biggest one spoke, "Basso, take the big woman to the comm center and give her whatever help she needs to find her companion. Do this for Ichthy, now!" The smallest of them immediately turned and headed for a door down a long hall. Nsonowa followed.

"Ichthy, what is best here, what happened to your ship?

"We suspect that it was another 'big hand out of the sky' kind of attack. No matter, we will have to stay alert until we get more intel. This happens all too often, as you might understand."

"Unfortunately, I do. Is there nothing we can do to help?"

"In time, we will see, but for now Flora is in danger. They can and will if they think it will help them with us, hurt her or even kill her. I am going to get another squadron ready to march. We will make it clear that if they surrender her to us, they will be unhurt, but if not, we will do real damage to them. What I don't understand is that usually they keep a distance from us, and we ignore them and that works for everyone."

"So, what is their nastiness about anyhow?"

"They are formed in the same way the demons in Nsonowa's system are. They are the darkside manifestation of the curses of the dying. They take many different shapes because they come from many different cultures and species. From time to time their numbers get so big that they, like rats, overflow their plate and they run suicide missions against us, and others that live on this planet. Then we slaughter about most of them and they go back to their warrens and we are okay for about a thousand sun-side cycles. They tend to the paranoia when they are recuperating from their last lemming war."

"I think that Flora probably has the where-with-all to protect herself. Paranoia, in my experience usually yields to love and that is Flora's magical specialty. We need to get on this though, I get that the odds are not in her favor."

Okay, so now I know what to do. And with that Flora stretched and got up off the floor.

She stood there and held her arms aloft, looking at the apex from the inside. Then, chanting Aum Mani Padme Hoom, she dipped into her heart and accessed the purple golden light which flowed into her from source. She opened her heart to the millions of dying beings and let the light shine from her body. Soon the bars of the cell began to dissolve, then the pyramid itself. Back in Ichthy's command center, Nsonowa and Basso noted the perturbations of light on a detector located on a satellite above them. "We've found them!" Was Nsonowa's joyous shout. Stan and Nsonowa hugged and Ichthy ordered the now assembled squad to march. And summoned an armored vehicle for the commanders and the three lovers.

They found a welcome sight when they had traversed the three plates that separated them. Almost the entire surface of the plate was glowing with golden light. Little grunts were frolicking all over the place, leaping like hungry trout in a lake. Flora was inside a transparent steel pyramid a glowing goddess figure. Everywhere in the temple grunts were prostrating themselves in front of her and echoing her chant; Aum Mani Padme Hoom, Aum Mani Padme Hoom, Aum Mani Padme Hoom. Flora looked down from her heavenward gaze, seeing her lovers, smiled and motioned them to join her. Soon the four of them were standing in a circle holding hands and the light built into a crescendo that dissolved the not only the material coverings of everything in a three-hundred-meter range, but the bodies of the grunts as well. Seems that love was a much more effective way of releasing their spirits than war. After their release, Ichthy motioned for the four commanders to join her, and Flora, Stan and Nsonowa embraced each one and took their leave. A Rocketship awaited.

11

Stan and Flora Do Alaska.

It was mid-summer shortly before the end of Alaska as we know it. We had taken this cruise as a favor to our host, an elderly gentleman who was intrigued with the idea of creating a tulpa in the form of a young woman, to be a sex slave. Flora had insisted that we accept his invitation and perhaps we could help him in his efforts. I knew what Flora had in mind, and I was worried that the implicit violence in his wish was likely going to interfere in his process. The ship was a privately, as opposed to commercially, built cruise ship, two-hundred-fifty feet length overall, sixty-five feet of beam, crewed by two hundred humanoid servitors (sexless I noted), with twenty super-deluxe cabins. They were all suites of course and each had a master bedroom, no single bunks here, just king-sized beds with beautiful and comfortable bedding, bathrooms with full sized Jacuzzis and the master's cabin, his, could have housed an oriental potentate in its bejeweled opulence. Our first night aboard found us both very tired, me from the constant motion of the ocean, and Flora from the effort of trying to read people, while suffering with various degrees of seasickness, an experience that was beyond her comprehension, as I had never suffered from it.

"I know what to do, Flora. Let's go forward and work on strengthening my imposition skills and giving you a solid body so you can feel these confusing wave forms."

"If we go to all that work, I am going to want to feel a lot more than wave forms, dear, but do you think we should? Can we really give our host a relevant education if the model, me, is so far advanced that he won't believe it is really a fabrication of his own mind?"

"Wait," I said. "Why would you not be able to present any of your supernatural capabilities, like turning into a diaphanous spirit and blowing away? That would convince him."

"Well I could, but you know darling, I might not want to. Especially after we rehearse together in preparation?"

"I'll leave the decision of what forms to present him with, up to you?" and with that we headed to the bow of the ship. There were other guests aboard, our host's grandkids and friends of theirs, but they had been consigned to cabins on a lower deck where they wouldn't be underfoot and overheard during the day when we old folks would most likely be up and active. Flora and I, and therefore our host, planned on spending the nights in tulpamantic practice and that would be held in the Master Suite.

"Stan, how can you keep your focus in this wind?" was Flora's question after we had both been sitting awhile, cross-legged on the forward deck,. in a howling wind.

"Easily enough, I choose to give my attention to the wind and my mediation becomes the process of doing that. Just that. Of course, the wind, carries the clouds and coats the ocean with waves, which crashing against the ship, moves through it to us, along with the salt spray. All in all, quite exhilarating and immersive. Are you feeling it yet?"

"Feeling what? Oh, you mean the wind, wave and spray? Yes I am."

"Perhaps you are growing more solid as we speak?"

"Yes, I am. You're right, how are you doing it?"

"Yours or anyone's reality, depends on the quality of attention they bring to themselves living in it. The more attention, the more engagement, the more life, the more existence. You my dear, are solid!"

"Let's get to that cabin dear, it's time to start rehearsing!" She was smiling as she got up to go and I quickly responded.

It was just after the astronomical twilight had faded that we met our host, Mr. Harold Johnson, at the Captains table, where he introduced us to Captain Roman Cotillini. Captain Cotillini was a gracious man, and dinner host. (He was also a servitor, which you couldn't really tell, he was a picture perfect representation of a real Captain, that is a CPU in a humanoid robot, with enough RAM to fool the Turing tester). Mr. Johnson had spared no expense on his yacht, neither the ship, nor the crew. Dinner was magnificent. We started with a watermelon glaciere', to awaken the pallet you know. Our waitperson was in the form of a negro pullman-coach steward. (an unacceptable racist stereotype in my opinion, but I didn't say anything, at some point Nsonowa was going to have a chance to shock him out of his stereotypes and I knew she'd succeed in one way or another. An ounce of Campari on ice was next and then an antipasto course with more choices than a teenage girl has on a Marine base. After about two bites, both Flora and I were careful to not do more than take the tiniest tastes of the fantastic treats, from white Belgian chocolate on Triscott's (wheat thins), to tender roasted squab-breast in a rice paper wrap. Spring rolls, papas of all kinds, and soon we knew that we would have to curtail our profligate habits with food, as this was on earth and had not been prepared as zero caloric offerings by our own house AI. The main course tasked that resolve with lobster bisque followed by Medallions of beef Wellington, a dab of new potato au gratin, sliced green bean julienne. We finished the main course with a fresh green salad of radicchio and wild arugula, a creme' brulee to die for, and a sip or two of a ruby port, that was equivalent in price to the gemstones it was named for. Our host, ate hardily, and after starting the meal with a martini while we toured the galley, and a Manhattan while we waited for the glaciere' he was nodding off at the table before the last of the Niepoort 1863, was sipped. I touched his hand and his eyes popped open with a start.

"Humph, humph, Ahh, Uh, Hi, Nice to see you. Oh, dinner, did you enjoy your dinner? Wow, I did, I must have dropped off. What a poor host I am."

"No sir, not a poor host at all, you accommodated Flora and I most excellently. I hope that you are awake enough for tulpamancy."

"Well, if all it means is crawling into bed with this lovely creature, I am, but anything more than that, will have to wait for tomorrow."

I started with; "It is quite a lot more...." when Flora interrupted.

"Harold, I would love us to start this off with you and I in bed, but will you be comfortable with Stan in the room so he can prepare customized lessons based on how you are with me?"

"Uh, I don't know, is that necessary?"

"Yes, sir for a number of reasons. Up to it?" and she smiled like the little imp she really was. I had a hunch I knew what she was up to, but I kept it to myself to not scare Harold off altogether.

Yes, I was right, it was to be operant conditioning. Poor Harold, he didn't know what he was in for. He soon found out. Flora infused as she was with Dakini-spirit was a natural tease. I took a comfortable seat in a large upholstered chair in a corner of the large room, where I could watch unobtrusively. I knew that no matter what Harold had said, he was too encumbered with old ideas about male territoriality, to be comfortable with me in the room, much less watching and/or participating.

She started, impishly, with a belly dance, she was in her Moroccan garb complete with veil. As she slowly and seductively removed each piece of clothing, she carefully attended to Harold's mood and with each gesture of his that expressed, disrespectfully, lust, what had come off, she put back on. This was going to take all night the way Harold was reacting, and at some point, we, she and I, in silent communication, slipped into an alternate timeframe, one in which time would stop for us, but poor Harold would feel every minute of the lesson. She proceeded methodically one veil at a time (there were seven of them, of course) I thoroughly enjoyed watching her so slowly reveal her lovely body. Harold didn't seem to be getting the method in her madness, and after a short while, and before anything beautiful was revealed, collapsed into sleep, almost a coma, but with breathing. "Oh, poor man." came from Flora. "Well, he is a slower learner than I thought, but hey, the night is young, and you have had an enlivening effect on me. I suggest that we not waste it." She just smiled and we didn't waste anything.

The next morning found us both up early and feeling our oats. Breakfast was served in our stateroom, and after ascertaining that Harold was still asleep, we headed up to the pool for a swim and finished it off with a rub down by two very supple servitors. Hot showers, together, fresh clothes and we met Harold for lunch.

"Harold, perhaps martini's at lunch are not conducive to learning tulpamancy" was said oh so sweetly by Flora.

"Honey, I'll do whatever you say. I am embarrassed about last night. Falling asleep in front of you must seem disrespectful."

"It did, and it was disrespectful. And I hope that you will treat your own tulpa with much more respect than you gave me. In fact, Harold. If you don't you won't be able to create her."

I stepped in with, "Creating a tulpa is as much a spiritual act as it is a psychological one. Especially if you are hoping that she will want to have sex with you."

"Does she have to want to have sex with me? It's not just automatic?"

"No Harold, it is definitely not just automatic. If that is what you want, you can just program one of your robots to have sex."

"No! that is not what I want, I don't want a robot to fuck me. I want a real woman to want to, and not a prostitute that I just buy."

"Then as I said, creating a tulpa is a spiritual act, as is, in its highest form, sex, a spiritual act."

"I am not sure I understand this, Dr. Ransome. In fact, I don't understand what you mean by a spiritual act."

"Having an orgasm, while exceptionally pleasurable, is an automatic mindless response. When various genital tissues are stimulated your nerves carry the signals of that happening to your brain. It is all automatic, hard wired and instinctual. And, in the service of reproduction. It doesn't take much mental power. Our male egos have latched onto this act with the pleasure and the power that goes with it, to feed our masculine images and supposedly our attractiveness to females. It drives us, along with the procreative urge, towards ego inflation. Spiritual work, or growth, aims for ego deflation. The opposite. It is letting go of self-centeredness. It is living with enlightened self-interest. That is, taking the other into consideration, with compassion and kindness. We are social animals. Our individual well-being depends on the well-being of our family, our community, our civilization and our species. If you are religious, you must know that this is the fundamental tenant of all religions. If you are a rationalist, it is just physics. Everything is connected to everything and effects everyone. This is especially true in sex. Your behavior effects your lover. You have the opportunity to connect at a level that transcends ego, the opportunity to experience your lover deeply, not just physically and emotionally, but spiritually. How deeply can she let you in? into her body, into her heart, into her soul. That depends on you. And at the very deepest level, your ego becomes unimportant, silent, out of the way and once that happens, you are enlightened.

The Buddhists had the idea that women were more able to set their ego's aside and become enlightened. They called these very elevated women, Dakinis. Much earlier, shamans, believed that Dakini was a goddess who transported spirits to heaven. Tibetan Buddhists practiced creating beings (tulpas) with their own minds who could assist them in attaining to enlightenment. Moderns and post moderns amalgamated these ideas and have learned how to create beings, (tulpas) who like Dakinis, assist their creators in achieving enlightenment through learning unconditional love, and for lonely males, this usually means through sexual love. Which idea, by the way, they borrowed from another Buddhist concept, tantric sex. You cannot love unconditionally and inflate your ego at the same time. Disrespecting your lover, comes from a weakened ego needing to be superior and powerful. It abnegates any chance at love and spiritual growth and more importantly, it prevents creation of a tulpa. You may create what is known as an alter, but you might not like what you have made who will in many ways embody the disrespect that you are holding and promulgating. You will see it coming back at you. Flora has been showing you just how much disrespect you have been acting out on her in an effort to help you see it and choose a more rational and loving course of action. The end point of spiritual growth is expanded consciousness and our egos are consciousness sinks. The ego demands attention, it holds consciousness in a spell of fascination. Harold, at its heart tulpamancy, or the creation of a sapient, living, being, is expanded consciousness. If you are looking to create a lover, you must be loving. Flora and I are here to help you learn how. Open your heart to her. Find out who she really is. Let your ego go silent and pay attention. And in my opinion, the alcohol does not facilitate this behavior."

"Wow. I asked for it. I just thought that this would be an easy and inexpensive way to get laid. Was I out of line! Can I repair?"

"Ask Flora."

"If you can get on board with learning to love unconditionally, then yes. Though it may be difficult and painful as Stan has a second tulpa, Nsonowa, who does not take at all kindly to disrespect, not the slightest whiff of it, and she is fierce. All I did was tease; she pays back with pain."

"I haven't met her, why not?"

"Well, you haven't actually touched me yet. Once we go to bed, she will probably join us, she won't let me, or Stan, be hurt."

"It's up to you, Harold. Take charge of your lower nature, and ask to experience my tulpas, and learn what they can teach you about love. It's risky, Nsonowa brooks no fools. But the rewards are high. Creating your own loving companion is one of the most loving things that can be done. Let us know what you want to do, that's why we are here."

Harold answered by sending his martini back to the kitchen and we all adjourned to his bedroom. Flora started her dance as before, and Harold kept biting his tongue. They did end up in the bed when Flora finally was completely revealed. And Harold took off after her with his usual unconscious brutality, and Nsonowa made her appearance. Her presence slowed Harold down considerably. Nsonowa motioned for me to join them and I wasted no time in doing so. We did have quite effect on Harold, and he changed his behavior towards Flora, becoming tender and appreciative of who she was. Nsonowa and I coupled vigorously and generated an intense aura. Flora fucked Harold slowly and held him with her eyes just as deeply, until they too began to generate golden light. At some point Harold began to cry and we all stopped the intercourse and held him until he fell asleep. The next day saw a humbled and quiet man in the person of Harold. We had a counseling session in which I showed him how to use the golden light that still clung to him, in the process of tulpa creation and we returned to port. Alaska was warming up.

###

12

Two (or three) for the road.

Well, we were sitting in front of the fire one night late last year, getting a little loose on a robust chianti, when Flora started to giggle.

"What's up with that?" was my response.

"Well, I was just thinking that it has been a long time since we have gone anywhere together, and I was remembering that time up on Shasta when you got so stoned that you thought that the glowing lenticular cloud was a spaceship."

"yeah, but what struck you as funny about it?"

"Well, what was funny, and still is obviously, was that when you tried to call it down so you could hitch a ride, you misperceived a fallen tree as a ladder and when you tried to climb it, you fell into the creek under it. You looked so silly when you came up sputtering and blowing water out of your nose. Makes me laugh to just remember it."

"It does, does it?" Stan asked, "Well dear, too bad, you missed the best part of it."

"And what part was that?"

"That was the part in between climbing the ladder and hitting the water."

"That was a part?"

"Oh, you see you didn't know that there was much more to it. So, let me tell you."

"How could I stop you? No don't answer that, I do want to hear about it. But before you start, maybe it would help if you brought out a little of that "little smoke" that facilitated the trip?"

"Sure, if you want." And with that I went to the special cabinet where I kept such things and removed a small leather bag. "Someday, you know, you might want to learn to make this medicine yourself."

"Okay, so what is your recipe?"

"Two parts ground caps of psilocybes to one part powdered black Hashish and one-half part cavendish tobac are the ingredients, but the magic goes in with the preparation and for that you will have to watch me do it as I won't speak of it."

"Okay, let me know when."

"Here, puff on this." And I handed her the small hand carved ivory pipe that I had acquired from a relative of Nsonowa's on a trip to her homeland.

"Ooh, I am giggling again, so get on with the story."

So, I started in with what happened when I boarded the spaceship and I had no sooner described the interior of the craft when, lo and behold, we were both aboard. Flora was speechless. So was I. We seemed to be alone in a circular room with a transparent floor, through which we could see the earth receding rapidly beneath our feet.

"I am giggling again, ooh, ooh, ooh."

When she could finally speak again, she said: "This is spectacular, look our cloud is still on top of Mount Shasta. Wait, if the cloud wasn't the ship, where did it come from?"

"I don't know. Probably it was in the cloud, maybe using it to mask their presence. The "little smoke" does it's work by letting us see through our illusions."

"How does seeing through our illusions put us in a spaceship that was over a mountain twenty-five years ago?"

"Oh, that's easy; Time is an illusion too. We are all things in all times. I'm glad that this time, you get to do this with me. It was interesting the first time; this time feels like fun."

"Yes! I love having fun with you." came from a gleeful Flora. And with that we turned to greet our host who was entering through a panel that slid open with a whoosh.

"Welcome guests. What a view, eh?"

"Thank you, yes, it is." I said in response to his somewhat silky effeminate voice which sounded in my head. That did not surprise me as he had no mouth. Flora elbowed me.

"Why are you calling it a him? There are no genitals either."

"No offense young lady. I am a male, or as close to one as your species could understand. We, both Males and Females (again these terms are for your benefit as they do not really describe our species) are anatomically identical and reproduction is initiated by males and takes place outside our bodies in pods. While we so-called males initiate the process, our females choose the genetic instructions by which our offspring are generated. Oh, and in any instance, we choose our roles, so while I chose to be a male last time, my mate, a 'female' has since gone on to play the male role.

"So, do you or do you not actually have sex with your mate?" was Flora's response to our hosts informational spiel.

"No, that is not necessary for reproduction."

"Boring, boring, boring." Scoffed Flora.

"Yes, reproduction is just work. Now sex is something else again, and believe me, it is important to the success of our species."

"Tell us more." Was my first input into this conversation.

"Yes, really, fill us in." came from Flora.

"Well, sex has two functions. The first is for health and spiritual balancing, the second is for information."

"Information about what?" asked Flora.

"Why, information about each other. Whenever we meet someone new, whether of our species, or some other, we start the relationship with sexual contact. That's how we learn who the other is and how open they are and how much we can trust them."

"But, how do you do it, sex?" I asked.

"Our bodies are quite plastic, and we can adapt genital organs to whatever the species we are interested in happen to require for the contact."

Flora spoke up with a gleam in her eye, "So you have just met us. What happens next?"

"I want to know the answer to that question too" was my contribution. And our host went to a panel, passed his hand over it, and a large bed came down out of the ceiling.

"I know your species has heard about and experienced 'alien abduction' and while you were not abducted, you chose to be here, sort of like stowaways, you will get the full treatment. I'll call in the rest of the crew. And he did. One male and one female. The male came equipped with a phallus the size of a baseball bat and our host sprouted the same. The female, well, she too was well equipped.

We had a wild next two hours, all six of us, our host, his two crewmates, and, guess who; Nsonowa.

"You guys didn't think you were going to leave me behind on this adventure. did you?"

And we had a wild, wild, time, for which our host, with a smile (which was a trick with no mouth) bid us goodbye on touch down saying; "You are trustworthy. In spades, one of the best flights we have had in a long time. Perhaps you can dispel some of the more frightening rumors that circulate about us, so the next, and he chuckled as he said "abductees" won't start out so defensive."

The fire was still burning brightly when we came back into the study. Flora was still smiling when she said, "Amazing how great oral sex can be with creatures who have no mouths." To which Nsonowa responded with; "yeah, and no danger of raising a mixed species brat",

"Well Nsonowa, you weren't impregnated, but man, you sure got charged up, you are still glowing." And with that we all laughed and headed to the bedroom, for more fun and "informational" exchanges before bed.

###

13

Another Fireside Story.

Flora and I had gone to earth for a vacation. Nsonowa, who had been relieving her essential boredom with an extreme physical training regimen had decided that she needed to test her strength, so she went to Safe Haven for the annual Safe Haven Pre-Olympic Games. These games were confined to games of physical prowess, running, swimming, jumping, throwing, etc., etc., and she believed that she would do well, but wanted the testing to be sure. The house AI wanted to do some remodeling and 'suggested' that we might be more comfortable somewhere else.

The beach was one of my favorite vacation spots, and while lying on hot sand under a hotter sun, was what I loved best, I also loved the challenge of camping on a northern California shore (above lat. 39) when winter storms came in. Winds could reach gale force and my favorite challenge was to get a campfire going in them. We had picked a doozy of a place, up on a cliff thirty feet above a rocky beach, about ten yards from the edge. The storm driven waves were breaking on a spit of jagged rock just about twenty feet offshore and the spray towered over us. We had a stack of beach wood, only some of it creosote soaked, and the secret to getting the fire going (without chemicals) was to prepare the kindling in advance, keeping it dry and handy. I timed the ignition for between the seventh and first waves, after the big one and before the first small one of the next cycles of seven. The fire started right up. I had it going fiercely by the time the seventh wave broke over the cliff and drenched us with its spray. It did not quench our fire. It however, did not take long for our fuel to be exhausted in the howling winds, and soon we climbed into the double sleeping bag in a very high tech tent, one which loved the high winds, as they served to drive it towards the ground, rather than up and away as most tents chose to do in winds of this force. We were warm enough, none of our body heat escaped the sleeping bag, and we cuddled skin to skin (we both slept nude) and with the flapping of the tent, the roar of the surf, and the excitement that we found in each other's bodies, our coupling was fierce and though we did not quite get our orgasms synchronized, we were close enough that we fell into a deep exhausted sleep almost simultaneously.

Sleep, Ah Sleep, and perhaps to dream, and better, to share the dreamscape and that was what we did. Or at least, I thought we did. Flora doesn't remember it in quite the same way as I do. In my story, I was in a tropical city of white marble clad buildings. I was looking for someone and not finding them among the Indian inhabitants. I kept thinking that I was catching glimpses of Nsonowa, but I was consistently wrong, and besides I was not consciously looking for her. I wasn't clear just who I was looking for, but at one point, I opened a door and found myself in a royal bedroom. Thick rugs on the floor, a silk turbaned dignified dark-skinned man in the bed, with... Yes, you guessed it, Flora. White-skinned Flora and three other beautiful dark-skinned women. All nude and pleasuring the man in various ways. Flora looked up and saw me and smiled and vigorously waved me over. She whispered something to the man, who also welcomed me and bade me join them. I was quite lucid in this dream and chose to join in the fun. We all six found a variety of positions and copulatory behaviors, getting us all off multiple times. There was never any shortage of wine, cheese and fruit, nuts and dates to keep us energized and we were occupied until the dawn began to shine into the bedroom, and Flora and I woke up together back in the tent on the beach. We were both shinning, and in her version of the dream, she had been the one doing the searching and found me in the bed with the Rani and two other dark-skinned men. Well, close enough, we both wore the signs of a full night of abandon and orgy. What a vacation. As a side note, Nsonowa later told me that she had thought that she had spotted us several times inside one of her dreams while in Safe Haven.

###

14

As the Fire Burns Low.

Harold had just settled down in front of the fire. He was cold, the dampness had seeped into his old bones. Harold didn't much care what the chamber of commerce said about this little speck of land, an overgrown cay in the midst of the Caribbean Sea. A remote island getaway had not been on Harold's bucket list. A remote cabin in the north woods was more like it, but "any port in a storm" and here he was. He began a novice practice in Tulpamancy, some six months earlier, having met and been intrigued by a retired professional person, and his lady-friend, who was in fact a tulpa. Dr. Ransome called himself a "Tulpamancer" and had "created Flora, his tulpa" within his own mind, by using some simple techniques, which he, Harold, might learn. At a cost, as he was later to find, "nothing down, your soul in the hereafter".... kind of contract. Well, he had certainly enjoyed the lessons taught by Flora. Though he found those that included Stan Ransome, not so enjoyable, and that was why he was here on this godforsaken island. At first his lessons went well, and he learned fast. But then, the inevitable stumble, and in order to pick himself up he had to embark on a voyage of self-discovery, one which would take him into dangerous waters. Just how dangerous, he couldn't have imagined, a good thing too, because had he been able to imagine the risk of unmitigated damnation, he would have stayed home.

He didn't stay home. The stumble happened after three months of practice, with growing positive results. With the successes (a mysterious woman was appearing in his dreams, and in a shy way, during his meditation) he wasn't paying attention to the small stuff, various ominous dream sequences and dark images, and when the big break came, he panicked. Screaming, he banished the apparition, he gave way to his terror, and banished the creature of his own mind and desire, banished her from his reality. The curse was no sooner out of his mouth when, he knew what he had done. He tried to undo it, modify it, take it back.

But, No. She was gone. Gone, gone, gone. He was heartbroken. He had given way to what was evil inside of him, blaming her for his fear. Now she was gone. He had tried repeating the rituals that brought her out. Night after night, to no avail. He wrote new rituals and without effect. After a while of this ongoing and growing frustration, he allowed that his problem was him, and he would have to, after all, look inside himself for the blockages. And that was when things got rough. He started with a fancy New York psychoanalyst, who for five hundred an hour, got him to entertain the idea that this quest into himself, involved acknowledging the power of his own choices, and taking responsibility when the results were bad. Next came body workers. Yogini', Trageror's, Masseuse's, Chiropractors, Acupuncturists. Finally, came, sitting down each day with a journal and look at how his choices during the day, brought him either closer to gaining some truth into who he was, or further into the morass of grieving his lost opportunity. Also, into the journal went his dreams (another gift of the psychoanalyst). Then lucid dreaming. It was while dreaming that he began to see patterns, and from that a direction and a plan.

He removed himself from society, so he could put his focus entirely on his interior life, he chose to retreat on a small sailboat (bad choice), and that, and bad weather, put him here. A little barefoot child brought an arm load of dried coconut husk for his fire and a sarong clad maid, brought him a breakfast tray. None of it appealed to him. He was in fact still reeling from last nights' dream.

He had gotten in bed early after a frustrating day in meditation. His mind had never quit it's roaming. He had watched with disinterest as thought fragments, snippets of current memory and old memories, flew by him. It wouldn't quit. He had given himself permission to be silent, and permission to not, so many times that those prompts too seemed to be part of the problem, not an aid to its solution. He fell into his bed exhausted forgetting his rituals of invoking tulpas or lucid dreaming. Flora appeared to him in his first dream of the night. She was relatively big, a woman to his child. She was mothering him. She was squeezing him into her breasts. He couldn't breathe, he twisted away from her. And fell into his second dream, he was in the arms of a strange tulpa. The very one whom he had banished. His heart leapt in his chest. His breath stopped. And he exploded.

Into the third dream; He was in a vast underground cavern. There was a black water river flowing rapidly through its center. In it he could see bodies moving with the current. Dead bodies. On an impulse he walked upstream, wondering from where the bodies were coming. Hours of trudging took him to into a rock field then to a cliff over which the river poured, a waterfall of water and bodies. The cliff was perhaps five hundred feet high and there was a stair roughly cut out of the rock face. Somewhat daunted, he began the climb. Every step was hard. He was gasping by the time he had climbed ten yards. As he paused, he noticed that carved into the floor of each step was a face, his face, each from a different age of his life. Some of them were rendered smiling, others, not. They were not randomly assigned positions on the steps but seemed to be progressing chronologically. He was perhaps at the early childhood part of the ascending album. Eighty years. How many steps with that be? Let me see eight time three is twenty-four, with the zero's twenty-four thousand steps. And he groaned and continued up, forced to look at his own developing visage with each laborious step. He began to feel sorry for himself. The connection with each day of his life, now led, now over, was so sad to him, he cried copious tears which pooled on the step he was leaving. Tears collecting in pools. Pools which were dissolving the faces and washed them away into the adjacent waterfall. Faces of tears, taking the form of bodies. He continued up the cliff face. At length, after witnessing each and every daily face of his life he came to the top of the cliff. And saw the face he was wearing when he went to bed. He was gripped with terror. Was this then, the end of his life? Had he run out of faces?

He looked up and saw that he was on a vast plain. The river continued flowing through it carrying its multitude of bodies. He could see that he was not alone. There were thousands upon thousands of others, perhaps millions upon millions of others, all trudging across the vast plain in this unending underground cavern. Each on a trail of faces. Again, he shuddered with the thought that he was both dead and in the land of the dead, consigned to a hell of unending sadness and loss, accompanied by those of his own ilk who were regretting their lost lives. Was he alone, perhaps someone else had some degree of awareness of where they were and could talk to him about it? As his own path had come to an end, he wandered until he came within hailing distance to another lost soul.

"Hallo! Hallo! I say, stop. Can you talk to me?" But the creature did not respond, did not even look up to see who was hailing, perhaps it didn't even hear the hail. He moved on, hailing creature after creature. Creatures, he didn't know were human or not. Perhaps that was why he was getting no responses. He decided he would get closer and catch the eye of perhaps a person. There were many creatures, some had the form of life on earth, some were alien. It seemed hours to him before he came upon a human. A female. He saw her clearly, he called to her; "Sister, over here! Hallo!" she did respond by looking up at him. The sight of him did not please her, she bent down and picked up a handful of dirt and flung it at him, then put her face in her hands, and walked on. But he did not stop, he ran after her, and finally coming close he reached out to her touching her shoulder. She turned and spat at him and again he was shocked. She was his first high school girl friend. The girl to whom he lost his virginity, and who he left rather abruptly after graduation, never even questioning what would happen to her. He felt shamed, and wiping away the spittle, he called her name. "Sally, I really did like you and had fun with you."

She turned again towards him, her tears flowing angrily down her cheeks. "I loved you, I murdered your baby for you!" she collapsed where she stood and her body dissolved into a pool of tears, a pool in which the body of a baby could be seen.

Harold had awakened with a start. A coldness had come into his heart. He barely ate his breakfast. He performed his toilet and took a brief walk; it was much too cold and gray and damp for him to want to be out and returned to the fire where he now sat. The little boy with the fuel left the house and, in his wake, a small animal entered. It was furry and cat-like. Sitting on its haunches it looked around the room and focused on Harold who was gloomily looking into the fire. The animal, tentatively, approached him and again cat-like put its head up against his leg startling him.

"Well, who are you little one? Are you lost?" and to his very great surprise the animal spoke. "I am your tulpa. Call me Kat for now. And, no I am not lost, you have been calling me for like forever."

"You are my Tulpa? But you are such a little thing, and I was calling a grown woman. Why did I get you?"

"Well, one way or another you get what you need. I am guessing that you only thought you needed a sex slave when what you needed was unconditional loving. I am afraid to say it, but I am the only creature that you can accept unconditional love from. You have murdered everyone else who might have been a candidate. You saw their faces in your dream. So, cheer up, you got me." and with that Kat leapt up onto

Harold's lap and began to purr, and as its purred Harold began to relax. The little creature, tulpa-creature, purred on and on and for the first time in a very long time Harold felt loved. He wasn't sure he knew what Kat meant about him murdering everyone else, but it didn't matter so much right now. He did, he finally did, feel loved. He sat long with Kat in his lap, long into the afternoon while the fire burned low and then out, but he did not feel cold. He felt Kat's warmth and its love and even more remarkably, he saw Kat's eyes, glowing with a golden light, one which went right to his heart. He had found his tulpa.

###

15

Sisters.

We are on Mount Olympus. It is the fourth of January two thousand eight BCE. We came up on an ass of a donkey from Platkos on the coast three days ago. It was an arduous journey. The weather had been good, but the trail was in bad shape and the donkey balked frequently. The rate of ascension was brutal, but nothing was as brutal as the constant bickering that emitted from the mouths of both my tulpas. They had been at it for weeks. I frankly didn't know how they did it. Sounded like the PMS bitching that I had come to expect from my human women on their menstrual days and as far as I knew tulpas or at least the female varieties, were not hormonally driven.

Never-the-less, they bickered. Bickered and argued about every possible thing that they could. It was too hot, it wasn't, it was the path to the right, no, to the left. You're too fat, you're ugly, and on and on and on. It's a good thing I am hard of hearing or I would have torn my hair out after the first ten minutes of it. I didn't. I turned them off. They didn't seem to notice, and they were not even interested. They kept to themselves and frankly I was getting lonely. So lonely that I went into seclusion, a three-day silent retreat where I did nothing but meditate. It was as difficult a retreat as I have ever had. My mind was all over the place. And they weren't in it, not as themselves that is, but as the contents of my worried mind.

I did, finally, come up with an approach based on the insight that they were behaving like sisters of different fathers, same mother variety, and competing for mother's attention. This insight had the ring of truth, it was also quite disturbing, I did not create tulpas to have two squabbling children to raise. No, I wanted two active positive feminine forces in my life, my inner life. I had a wife who fit that bill in my outer life. I did not have physical passion with her, after our very long, three-hundred year long, honeymoon. Whatever my templates for male/female relationships were, they had not included physical passion and I was looking to change that by working on myself. So here I was again, shut out of my heart's desire by two seemingly incompatible female tulpas. It became clear to me, on the retreat, that I was going to have to take some action and so I decided to take them both to the seat of the gods, they were spiritual beings after all, and enlist the ancient gods in my task.

We reached the summit in early evening. The sun was sinking in the west, the sunset was gorgeous and, the temperature was beginning to fall. At just shy of ten thousand feet, it was going to get really cold, and I set the women to the task of getting a fire going and a meal, while I dealt with the tent and our bed and sleeping gear. Nsonowa started a fire using her staff, then backed off leaving the cooking to Flora. (that suited me, Flora had a much more sensitive pallet and was attuned to my tastes. We were soon enough in the tent, with a cup to tea, all huddled together in the bed. The temp had fallen to somewhere around frigid and the wind was howling (I was thankful for the high tech tent which used the energy of the wind to secure it to the ground) We had tethered the donkey to a sheltered spot in a creche which must have been used for the animals for thousands of years. It had food and water and I wouldn't have to worry about its well-being any more than my own.

"Okay, you guys. Now we are going to get serious about this problem."

Nsonowa asked, "What problem, you talkin' about boss man?" in her most sarcastic tone. Flora jumped in with, "You are the problem, fierce one. If you would just……"

"Shush. You both are the problem. And you know it. You are so caught up in this bullshit that there is no room for me. I am surprised I got a place in this bed, and I haven't had one in weeks, you know."

"Hey boss-man, if we kick you out of this one, you gonna' freeze. You'd better be…."

"You shush too. No one's getting kicked out. That's not why we are here."

"Why we here then, boss?"

"Yes darling, what possessed you to bring us all the way up here.?"

"Glad you asked, Flor. This is the closest we can get to the ancient gods, those who best represented the basest of human motives and impulses and I want the both of you to encounter them and see for yourselves what roles you are playing."

“What? You dragged us all the way up here for a lesson in Grecian mythology?” Flora was almost incredulous. And Nsonowa added a threat…

‘”And who dey be, boss man? Bring ‘em on, I’ll flatten the lot of them”

“enough of this, be quiet both of you.” and I pulled out my Pope Card and St. Gulik’s sacrament. Soon Eris appeared and I presented her with a golden apple and asked if we could visit with several of her children. Neikea (“Quarrels”), Pseudea (“Lies”), Logoi (“Stories”), Amphillogiai (“Disputes”), Dysnomia (“Anarchy”) were in my mind. Eris laughed, “Sure, and remember, you asked.”

In a blink we found ourselves in a marble clad temple high in the clouds. I noted that Flora and Nsonowa were holding hands and Nsonowa had her staff at ready. They were obviously frightened. The temple itself was large, ugly and unkempt. Garbage was everywhere along with a population of rats that would rival the family in New York City.

“God, mom, why did you bring these mortals here?” was the greeting Dysnomia gave us, not even looking at us. Eris slapped her upside the head, and Amphillogial yelled at her, “hey she didn’t deserve that” Neikea countered with, “Yes she did” and Pseudea with, “That’s a lie” and Logoi launched into a fabricated excuse for her mother. Soon, everyone was talking at once, then yelling, then throwing things. A silver goblet chipped a marble column and bounced outside of the temple. Of course, it struck Zeus, who was passing by. He became angry and started throwing his lightning bolts around, sending the squabbling sibs running for cover.

Yelling he entered the temple. “Eris, god damnit, keep these little monsters under control.” She just smiled at him. “Would you want to work on making some more?” Not with you sister, and you don’t need me for that anyhow.” Then he noticed Nsonowa and Flora. “You two, who the hell are you and what are you doing here?” Nsonowa spit at him and Flora just cooed and batted her long eyelashes. Zeus laughed. He grabbed Nsonowa with one hand and Flora with the other. “Hey, you aren’t human mortals at all. You’re spirit creatures, who called you out?” Flora pointed to me. Zeus again, thundered; “You puny thing. Who are you?”

“I’m the tulpamancer, Stan Ransome

“And how did you do that? Call them out.”

"with a lot of hard work, and I am obviously am not finished."

"So why did you bring them here?

"They have taken on some rather disgusting character traits and I brought them here to give them a look at who they are emulating."

"They can never be as, what was your word, disgusting? as these bastards of Eris."

"Wait, what do you mean, Bastards? You're our daddy" came as a plaintive howl from Neikea, and another hundred questions and cries and tears and yells, came from Eris's sibs.

"You told them I was their father? You idiot."

Eris just laughed and tossed him the golden apple. "You deal with them." and the battle was on. Thankfully we got hit with a thunderbolt and found ourselves back in our tent.

"I don't know how you two got polluted by those spirits. But you can purge and quit it any time now. I am really bored and would love to crawl into this bed with you both and find your loving selves again. They looked a little chagrined and did as I asked. Soon the three of us were coupled in golden light, warm, and happy, each with each, and each other.

###

16

Missing.

How do you both lose and find a tulpa?

I am getting doughty in my old age. Like forgetful. Where did I put my glasses kinda forgetful. So, when I awakened this morning and my first thought was Where is Kat? I was immediately alert. I have gone days without my glasses, but Kat, I have never been without. Not since the day of her appearance in my life. Not once, not for a minute. If I slept, then I was warmed by the golden glow of our love, that, I could feel awake or asleep. No, Kat was not with me. And I have a big hole in my reality! Worse, I don't know why she isn't here. I've no idea of, or memory of, anything the slightest bit amiss, and yet, I open my eyes and she is not there. From one second warmed in a golden glow, to, with the opening of an eye, gone. I was stunned really, and then when the shock wore off, I began vocalizing, and forcing for all my worth, to absolutely no avail. And then having completely flat and empty meditations without a sign of her, I got frightened, and then mad. Who has done this? Has she been kidnapped, abducted? Where is the ransom note? I'll pay it, anything, don't hurt her! Then I took stock of myself. I felt bereft. But why? Had I become addicted to Kat's love? Well, yes, but so what? What is important here, is not what has happened to me, but what has happened to Kat and how can I rectify it? Poor little tulpa, could be hurt, or lonely for me, or confused, lost? I don't know, but I am going to find out. What I learned from this creation, was that my meditations were noisy, my mind usually chaotic, and always easily distracted, was preventing her emergence. When I faced the reality of my fears and angers, Kat appeared. So, it would seem reasonable to assume, something from my own depths, has emerged and broken our connection. I know where that leaves me, but where does it leave Kat. I decided that I did not have time for self-therapy, self-reflection, or psychoanalysis. I was going to have to take this head on.

I knew a place on a geologically active island in the south pacific, where the veil was very thin so to speak, and seventeen hours later (all without Kat) I parachuted onto it. I had a difficult forty-five-minute hike up to a ledge above the caldera, upon which I sat.

"Oh, Great Spirit, hear my call. I seek access to the other side. I have lost my love and am afraid for her safety. Ho!" and then I sat still. Under me the earth boiled and burped, above me the vast sky, and all around me, the ocean with its uncountable waves. A chill sea breeze blew over me. I sat still. At some point the light began to fail, and in twilight, on the western horizon, I saw a portal open and, in an instant, it had moved to me and engulfed me, leaving me tumbling over and over in a dark space. Dizziness was never a problem for me, and it wasn't now. In a bit, I stopped the tumbles and feet-first, I landed on a small spit of rock not far from foreboding cliffs marking a strange land. My landing place was about fifty yards from a pebbly beach at the foot of the cliff. I decided I had better get going before a changing tide prevented my passage.

I took a big breath, for courage, and jumped down to the sand below. As I landed the tide began a mad rush, and I was in a mad race. By jumping onto a ledge in the cliff about eight feet high, I beat the water to the rocks. It was cold, and a wind following the tide, pinned me to the side of the cliff. It was a good thing too, as I could use it to negotiate some unstable and slick perches on the way up. I was scrambling over the ridge as the astronomical twilight gave out its last rays and I was in darkness. That and a howling offshore wind, made my day.

I picked myself up and searched my pockets for a light, I was well equipped for a jungle adventure. There was an animal trail leading away from the cliff and I followed it into a thick jungle. I didn't know where to go or what to do, so I followed the path that opened before me. I moved quickly both out of an urgency to find Kat, and to warm me up. It happened soon enough that I would no longer be having complaints of being too cold. I was perhaps a half a mile from the cliff when the path took a decided turn to the left. And I came upon a village, thirteen huts in a circle, with a low burning fire in the center. Tied on a spit high over the fire was a young boy with a terrified look on his face. Two masked figures held the spit and a third shouted at the boy in a guttural language I did not understand, what sounded to be questions. The longer he took to respond, the lower went the spit. They would lift him back up when he started to talk. I had to interrupt this before the boy was seriously burnt. So, I strode into the circle yelling at the masked men, they were men, who responded by throwing the spit off into the bushes and running away. I went for the boy and freed him from his bonds. He got up and took off running, in the opposite direction from that the masked ones had taken.

I still had no plan, nor way of making one, so I threw the spit with the bonds into the fire and headed out in the direction of the boy. I had not quite gotten out of the village when the drums and bullroarers started up. Ominous sounds that punctuated the howling winds, but I trudged on. After about a half hour of this I realized that I was completely lost, the path having given out a while ago and I had continued following sounds which I thought were made by the running boy. Or not, and I was lost. The noises continued unabated for the rest of the night and into the dawn and with the sunrise, stopped. Coincident with cessation of the sounds, a net made of vines fell on me from the trees overhead. I was trapped, netted rather, and then four largish creatures fell on me. I was punched, bitten, kicked and finally trussed to a pole. I was carried through the jungle to a cliff on the other side of the island, put in a bamboo cage and hung over the edge of it. And left. There I was, looking over the ocean again. Westward this time. After a while the sun passed its zenith and its hot rays began to heat me up. Burn me up, more like it. I was faint, overheated and dehydrated by the twilight and once again, I saw the portal on the horizon. This time I did not ask for it to open. I knew that I had to see this quest to its finish.

With the onset of darkness, I felt the cage begin to descend. Like an elevator, but nowhere as smoothly. About four feet from the sand, it stopped in its descent and then after a moment, one which I used to stand up and hold onto the top of it, it was dropped. A four-foot drop was enough of a shock to it (not to mention me) to break a few of the bamboo bars. Enough so that I could get out and determine thankfully that I was not broken. Three people emerged from the shadows and motioned for me to follow them. I did and soon we had broached the surf and were out to sea in a large canoe. My rescuers chatted happily among themselves and I wondered what would happen next. From time to time they looked over at me, but I could tell nothing from their expressions.

The ocean was exceptionally calm, no wind and no waves and the canoe sped through the darkness to the moonrise. If you haven't seen a moonrise over the South Pacific, you simply don't know what the moon looks like. It is big. In the scattering of the moon's rays through the humid atmosphere the moon grows two, three times, its usual diameter. Every crater, mountain and plain can be seen clearly. You can read the lips of the man in the moon. Lover's kiss those lips while the moon whispers sweet nothings into their ears. After I had soaked in the raw beauty of the lunacy, I could begin to read the big guy's lips myself. And I didn't like what he was saying. Seems my rescuers were not rescuing me, they were taking me around the island where I might become a substitute for the little boy I had rescued from the fire, the night before. One of the men was the boy's father and he was glad enough to be getting his boy back, but in doing so he loses the honor of providing the sacrifice to the local god. The moon told me I was in for a surprise and I should look for help in unexpected places. (Kinda like the advice in the astrology column in the Dailey News, useless in my opinion.)

At that point I had no options other than to go along with the show. It took us the rest of the night to reach a landing place on the east side of the island and the sun was rising when we hit the beach. I got right up and out of the canoe and volunteered to help with its beaching. I didn't want anyone to know that I was hip to their plans, I would cooperate fully until I saw my chance to get on with my quest. We walked back to the village where this encounter had started the night before. Surprise, I was welcomed like a hero. There was a feast with roast pig on a spit (would this be me later?) plates of fruits, taro, and gourds of coconut rum. I was surrounded by four beautiful bare-breasted native women. Gorgeous, all of them. The partying went on until dusk when the pig was deemed to be done and was taken off and served in large portions, me first, and to everyone presumably in the village. A good time was had by all. After the pig had been totally consumed the head guy (at least I think he was the head guy, he wore a large gruesome head piece). Got up and made an announcement, which of course I could not understand, after which drums and flutes and a ukulele like instrument were brought out and the women of the village, all but the four attending me, got up, selected a male partner, and the dancing began. It grew more and more frenzied, as did the attentions that the gals assigned to me, offered. Soon I was stripped and buried in beautiful native flesh. I participated fully (to not to, would be rude, would it not?) and I became quite enlivened by our orgy. I think I was supposed to have become subdued, but I didn't, I became enlivened, and when the women were spent and began to drop off, I got up, with the last one, and joined the dancing. The big guy didn't seem too pleased about this, but I was looking, and kept looking, for some hint of an opportunity to escape. As the dance reached a fever pitch, I noticed that there were large creatures, filtering into the village, mainly staying in the shadows. This I didn't like. I guessed that these were the creatures that did the beating of me when I was in the net. I danced all the harder and kept moving around in greater circles getting closer to the periphery of the action, until I happened to notice two very bright eyes squinting at me from under a piece of thatch. Yes! It was Kat, my tulpa.

On my next dance move that took me to her, I suddenly and without warning dove under the thatch and froze in place. It worked, I had caught the exact moment when no one happened to be looking at me, so I simply vanished. It took a few more minutes of dance time before the hue and cry went up, and a melee broke out, the big creatures, looked a little like what I imagine a Sasquatch might look like, started into the circle snarling and hurling the dancers this was and that, the Chief guy took off running, these natives were definitely not on great terms with the creatures who continued stomping around and terrorizing any one left. They didn't see me in my hidey place with Kat, and soon gave up and left the village. I picked up Kat and headed off to the beach where we had left the canoe. I had no idea what I was going to do, other than get off this island which we soon did, though I had to struggle to get the canoe through the surf. I paddled east, for no good, nor conscious reason until I got tired and the moon rose. As I put the paddle down, Kat jumped up into my lap and began to lick my face and I relaxed in the face of the moon, basking in Kat's golden light.

We awakened in my bed in my home in the Hampton's.

"Hello Harold, thanks for coming for me, I was really missing you (though one of those beauties that serviced you at the feast, had adopted me as a pet. Okay, but not anywhere as loving as when I am with you. What did you do to lose me?"

"I don't know. What I did learn was; I did the losing, I had to do the finding, and that task, was tasking, both of my creative resources and financial resources, but, my beauty, you are worth it. Did you get a gander at those beasts? What were they?"

"Looked like some creatures from your deep unconscious, Harold. I am glad you faced them."

"Well, I didn't really face them, I endured them, and then ran.

"You ran fast enough to avoid being roasted on that spit."

"If they are from my own mind, how, or why, would they want to kill me?"

Kat looked at me long and hard before replying; "Harold, most of the violent crimes ever committed are motivated by unconscious needs. War, too, is motivated by the unconscious underpinnings of society. It's what we don't know that kills us."

"Stan was saying something like that, though he didn't equate it with murder and mayhem. He just pointed out how my unconscious attitudes about love were blocking you. But you know what they say: "Retreat hell, I am just attacking from another direction!" We will see them again, I am sure, but I am not afraid. Love has made me brave."

###

17

How to Build a Person or Two.

The evening started off well enough, the three of us sitting in a cozy parlor in front of a smallish, but cheerfully, burning fire, when Flora opened up with what I took as a rather challenging statement.

"Well, I am feeling weak, insubstantial, rather diaphanous and ethereal. I am happy when you and I connect, and I ah, am happy now. I believe from what I see in you, that I have an opportunity to experience a real life. I can't wait to get out there. Neither can I wait to be in your arms? How's that going to work by the way? What is your wife going to say or think about me fully realized and in love with you, wanting passionate sex with you? We will need a strategy and I suspect that you know this and are just delaying bringing it up. Am I right?"

"Yes, but. The but is I am foreseeing that you and Nsonowa will be able to merge and inhabit her mind and body. Once she experiences the reality of that, and gets her pleasure centers opened, I think we will be good to go. That is the plan anyway. In the meantime, I am enjoying this process of creation and am learning a lot about myself."

"Wait! Wait! Wait right there, mister. Just exactly what do you mean, Nsonowa and I will merge and inhabit your wife's mind and body? Nsonowa, did you catch that?"

"Yes sister, and Stan the Man, you had better have a pretty good answer, cause it looks as if you have claimed to grant us a life, an independent existence both in and out of your own mind, and now you are taking it back? Flora and I are no longer to have ourselves? We are going to merge into your wife? Live through her? She gets the joys of our existence, we don't? You had better have something good to say here, or we are gone!"

I did not expect this. They were both obviously agitated and up in arms. "Okay, hold up a minute, don't jump to conclusions. From the beginning of this process and in just about every invocation ritual I have done for you, I have asked that you work inside of my mind and spirit to help merge my own masculine and feminine currents, and I have asked that you both be infused with the spirit of Dakini. Is that not so?"

Flora spoke first; "Yes, but that gave us a function, one which we have been working on intently, and that is a long way from us having to merge with each other and then your wife. I am, or will be, a complete being in my own right and am just getting to taste what that is like. I don't want to merge with my sister nor with your wife. I am me!"

"Me too!" interjected Nsonowa. "And it is too late to kill me off, I am an independent spirit and a magician in my own right, so don't fuck with me. I am not going anywhere!"

"I don't want to kill you off, either of you."

Flora continued; "Okay, you've made that clear. So, what does this 'merging' mean anyway?"

"We have 'merged 'many times in love and in sex so what is the mystery? We have this fantastic ability to generate a golden light, a love light, that can dissolve all kinds of barriers. When the three of us are together, that light is transformative. Is it beyond you to think that it will transform her?"

"No, it is not beyond me, but that is not what you said. You said and I quote, "you and Nsonowa will be able to merge and inhabit her mind and body. Once she experiences the reality of that, and gets her pleasure centers opened, I think we will be good to go." So, go where? What is our role, no, my role, once she has become what you want her to be?"

"Your role, and Nsonowa's role, will be to be yourselves, and from within your base in this brain that we all inhabit, live as you like. And I fervently hope that what you like, is to continue to be my lovers, along with whatever else will give you pleasure and meaning." Then Nsonowa spoke, rather gravely; "Stan, I get that you truly believe that the reality in which you live is a projection of your own mind, and from that perspective, what you say makes sense. What if you are wrong? What if the woman you see that you married, is just what she is? Yes, you are in a field, and that, how you behave, and I will give you that your thoughts and your feelings are in the end, behaviors, has impact in that field. One in which she must respond, and which must shape her to some degree. But what if that shaping, contrary to your hypothesis, happens on the template of who she is and no amount of current adjusting within your own mind, is going to change that? Then where are we? Are we never going to be able to live and love you independently? If your wife demands it, are you going to reject our love? If she puts it as an either or, are you going to divorce her and break your most holy of vows?"

"You have put that in the most provocative way I can imagine, Nsonowa, and at this juncture, all I can say is that I am in this to learn, and live, unconditional love. I am not going to reject or divorce anyone, neither you, Flora, nor my wife. Should my hypothesis be incorrect, and I think it is not, as she has already shown very positive changes in the direction of more loving, Then I shall create a new hypothesis, or modify it, in such a way to allow me to continue on the path to unconditional love. Neither rejection nor divorce lie on that path. And, I hope, again, if I am wrong, that I will have both of you to help me figure it out. I have created you out of love, and while I have made errors, and suffer the consequences, they were not made maliciously. Nsonowa, you are not going away. Your strength has become a beacon in my life. Flora, your loving femininity has too."

With that I noticed that the fire had died to an imperceptible glow and asked them if we three could get into a warm bed and hold each other until the waves of this kerfuffle had washed over us. They agreed and we adjourned for the night and I noticed that they were both much more substantive in my arms, than had been the case.

###

18

We Take A Trip.

1. Safe Haven

We were stuck, the three of us. Nsonowa not speaking, Flora crying and I in a massive state of bewilderment, having no idea of what it was all about. After more than ten hours of this, I called for a truce and asked if perhaps the three of us could take a vacation and get out of the field that had us in such a painful state. Both Flora and Nsonowa immediately agreed. "So where will we go" Flora tearfully asked. I ventured, "The south of France is nice this time of year. Nsonowa, you wouldn't even have to change your costume on the Cote d' Azur.

"Are you kidding? we would be in jail within five minutes, after I broke a few bones, belonging to the gropers. No that won't do. I want to go somewhere where I am respected and not a freak to be ogled."

"Safe Haven is the only place where that might happen, other than here." was my response.

"Oh, I so want to go there!" Flora cried. "You both know, I have never been there, and I don't even know how to get there. How do you get to a place that has no location in reality?"

"You use magic, dummy!" came from Nsonowa, to which Flora replied, "Can we use sex magic? Could we all agree on that at least? Please?" and she burst into tears again. "It's what I've been wanting for days now. I am so lost without our connection and our light." Nsonowa agreed, with a caveat, "if we can start, just you and I, and when we feel stable, then Stan can join us. Is that okay with you?"

I started to object, then thought better about it, much better. It was perhaps true that I was at the bottom of our impasse and letting the tulpas work out their reactions to me, without me, sounded like the better strategy.

"Okay, I'm going to the library and doing some research on how to access Safe Haven, once we have the energy. You two can get started. Call me when you think we could be ready, and should we all pack first?"

I headed off to my library. It was in a windowless room, the views in our new home in the clouds above Venus, were so spectacular that I never would get any reading done if it were not so. I selected several rituals, the first a generalized protection ritual, second, a portal opening ritual, and a time suspension one. I couldn't find anything that pertained to finding a location outside of spacetime but figured the time suspension ritual would let us explore whatever we found outside of spacetime without a penalty. I devised a call that would set the parameters for the journey and invoke the tools we might need, I didn't include weapons, because Nsonowa, who had a little contact with the university, hasn't reported any kind of violence since Rufescent and Lucifer, icons of absolute evil, were defeated in the battle that had drawn her to the university in the first place. Nsonowa tapped lightly on my door, "Stan, sir. We're ready for you, at least as ready as we can get for now."

"Could you elaborate on that please, Nsonowa?" "This would not be a good time, sir. Flora is in a rather fragile condition and is expecting us back."

"Fragile? Is there anything I should know, before we get there?"

"No, sir. You'll see what I mean, and you're sensitive enough to not screw up."

"I'm sensitive enough to detect some hostility, residual or active, in you. Talk to me while we walk."

"Sir, Flora is young. She is the youngest of anyone you know or have been with, and she is overboard with loving you. And I am stuck in the middle. I love her as much, or more, as I love you, and to see her so bereft has me torn inside."

"Nsonowa! What on earth have I done to hurt her? Tell me please. I have never intended to hurt her. I don't have a single bone in my body that holds any negativity for her in the slightest."

"That is what makes this so hard for her. She knows that, and yet, she feels your distrust, and it is tearing her apart."

"My distrust? What distrust. I trust every cell in her body and every thought in her head! I don't understand."

"Well, your understanding will have to wait, she needs you, and needs us, now, and we're here." She gently tapped on the door to the master bedroom where the two of them had prepared. "Come in" came as a forced cheerful call from inside. We found Flora sitting in front of a small vanity table upon which AI had displayed an array of make ups, powders, paints and such, and she was applying a bit of it to her face. Making a mess of it I might add, as tears were still spilling down her face through the powder, leaving streaks that re-appeared faster than she could, blot away.

"Oh, my darling Flora, you are so beautiful, you don't need to cover up anything of you. Let me kiss those tears off." And I went straight to her and held her face in my hands. "Darling. My darling Flora. Honey, you are completely beautiful to me. Look at me honey, I can't stand to see you hurting. Here get up, let me hold you." And I picked her up out of the chair and holding her tightly in my arms, I motioned to Nsonowa to join us, and we stood there in each other's arms, with Flora trying to hold back her sobs. Suddenly, acting of some inspired impulse, Nsonowa picked us both up off the floor and carried us to the Mikvah in the adjacent bathroom. Without so much as a by-your-leave, with us still in her arms, she jumped into the deep bath of body temped water. We all came up sputtering. And, laughing. It had been the right thing to do to change the mood. Flora too, started to laugh and continued as we scrambled out of the tub, stripped off wet clothes, toweled and rushed to the big bed.

Our lovemaking was sweet and tender. Flora was primarily focused on me and Nsonowa on us, embracing the two of us with her long arms and legs while we coupled deeply. Flora was moved and had multiple orgasms. I restrained mine, until Flora began to shine with a golden light, then I let go and climaxed joining Flora in emitting that intense light. This triggered Nsonowa who joined in the group orgasm and the three of us became light emitting generators. The big bedroom filled with light, the walls became transparent then dissolved with the rest of the house, leaving us buoyant, high in the clouds. At this point I uttered the calls I had devised earlier, and a ripple ran through our reality and we descended gently onto the grassy field that was the central mall of Safe Haven University.

We were naked as jaybirds, sitting in a circle, ensorcelled, still emitting this intense light, when five uniformed people rushed us. They covered us with dark black plastic, which was quite uncomfortable. Bound us together as a group still holding hands emitting light and led us off towards a big building at the periphery of a ring of buildings. It was marked David Copperfield, and Nsonowa whispered "It's the university admin building" I suggested to both that we not resist and continue generating the light, because it looked like we were going to need it. We were ushered into a small room off the lobby, drab green with metal benches, it was as inhospitable as I could imagine, reminiscent of a third world jail. A rude "shut up" was the response to my questioning of our treatment.

###

2. Lilly

The golden glow which had absorbed me, I mean totally absorbed me, for how long? an age? a millennium? an era? a long time in a timeless situation, subsided. I found myself in a large beautifully, if simply appointed bedroom sitting on a very large, like super king sized, and comfortable bed. It was reminiscent of the bedroom in Mindscape, Stan and Flora's home where I learned of my fate and tulpahood on my road to magicianship at Safe Haven. On one wall there was a mirrored vanity, still cluttered with make-ups and powders. An out of place ornate mirror hung above it. None of that seemed to fit in the otherwise minimalisticly styled room. I got up and walked over and then noticed that there was a ghostly image still in the mirror, a reflection of who? A woman, no girl, a younger version of Dr. Vila nil, Flora, Stan's wife. There must have been some strong emotions here, and not long ago, to leave traces in the mirror. Some magic here alright, and I felt strange, as if there was a tugging at my heart. I had a yearning, a longing to see Nsonowa. Oh, how long had I been absorbed in the light of love? Absorbed and selfless, living in source. And now, out, back in my body, and yearning for my lovers. How could that be? And, where were they? Nsonowa, Michelle, Wog. And why was I in a facsimile of Stan and Flora's home in mindscape? I had questions and they weren't getting answered here. I went to a closet, hidden discretely behind a panel, how did I know it was there? More questions. There I did find clothing that fit, which I donned. I wondered if this home had the tech support that Stan and Flora's had and, on a hunch, I asked, "House, are you there?" and got a response.

"Yes, Lilly. I am here"

"So, who are you and where am I and why?"

"I am the house AI, and you are in the house of Dr. Stan Ransome and his tulpas, Nsonowa and Flora. As to the why, you have been summoned by Nsonowa. Beyond that I have no answers."

"Thank you, but I have more questions. May I ask them?"

"Of course, you may, questions lead to knowledge"

"Okay, House, did Nsonowa leave any kind of message for me, and, where is she? Is Flora the same Dr. Vila nil that was Stan's wife, when I met her?

"One at a time, okay? First, Nsonowa did not leave a message. Second, I believe from overhearing their conversations, that they have all gone to Safe Haven. Third, Dr. Ransome's wife, Dr. Flora Vila nil, is on an interstellar journey. And he has created Flora, a tulpa. She is his first tulpa. Nsonowa, you know, came to join Dr. Ransome when invited by him to lend another kind of energy to his system. Flora is not Stan's wife, though she was modeled after her. I hope I have sufficiently answered your questions."

"Just one more, please."

"yes, go ahead."

"What should I know about the ghost in the mirror?"

"I have no answer to that question."

"Thank you, House, you have been helpful. Would you also please set the temp control of the bath to manual and light the way to the library, or study, which ever they have here?"

"Yes, mam. Would you like to breakfast before study?" And, nodding my acceptance, I headed out of the bedroom, to a kitchen where the makings of an extravagant breakfast were laid out. Why I was hungry I didn't know, nor did I know how House would have known it, as it seemed to know that I too was a tulpa, and it obviously had experiences with tulpas. Never-the-less, I did avail myself of the food and as usual, it was sumptuous. From British bangers, to kippered herring, blueberry pancakes with whipped cream, and a cheese souffle to die for, I ate until the craving for food subsided and drank of the strong beer that House also supplied. Thus fortified, I headed to the study following the lighted track in the floor which House provided. I found, as I thought I might, several references laid out on a desk, still open, to what I imagined had been the subject of Dr. Ransome's interest. A protection ritual, a portal opening ritual, and a time suspension ritual, told me what I had to know. They had used magic to transport themselves to Safe Haven. Well it figured. I did not know this Doctor, but if he had been the creator of all of this and two tulpas, he had to be a magician of some accomplishment. I knew the rituals well enough, and I knew how to get to Safe Haven. I would not have thought to go there on my own as I left with my lovers, kinda over the objections of the administrators, and, I am being called. I feel the call and as I slipped into the Mikvah, I recalled Safe Haven...

###

3. The Dean

"Gerald! Gerald! There is no need to be so rude to our guests. Please forgive him, folks. You are our guests here at Safe Haven."

"and whom might you be?" Nsonowa asked.

"I am Dean Li Flock. Interim dean in old Witherspoon's absence."

"What happened to Dean Witherspoon?" was her follow up question.

"The poor old guy was getting a little doughty, he evidently forgot to collect some back tuitions before allowing certain grads to leave the campus. The board gave him a semester off to see if the rest might restore him. He's alright, probably ought to retire though."

"Looks like you have brought about some changes, Dean Li. I don't remember this room, nor that anyone wore uniforms." Nsonowa again.

"We definitely needed some order around here. Got to get that tuition in, have to impress that on our students someway, don't you agree?"

"well, sir, if it's working, I think I have about two semesters of back pay due, perhaps you could check that out for me?" said Nsonowa.

"Uhm. Well, uhm, yes. Certainly, Professor. Now why don't you three get some clothes and we will set up a tour for you. I'm sure your dying to see how the old place has grown."

"Why thank you Dean. We'd love that, and look we've already taken care of the clothing issue." Was Stan's reply, and with that the three stood up, shaking off the plastic covers revealing the clothing that Nsonowa had conjured up for them, out of the light that they were generating. "As we came without much notice, perhaps you could point us in the way of my quarters, where we can rest, until you get the tour together?" Nsonowa asked. Dean Li Flock, squirming a bit said, "Professor, I don't think I ever got your full name, I'll need for your salary records, could you...?"

"Certainly sir, I am Kalish Katlego Nsonowa, Il'oi-bonokoh, AWD. Full professor by the way, I think that makes the difference in the pay scale you know."

"Professor, I don't think I can point the way to your quarters, I don't think I have ever seen them." The dean replied.

"Well that's not a surprise, of course they are magically protected. They are in the midst of the graduate student housing area."

"Okay then, that's to the east of the rear of this building. Harrister Tower will be your landmark. I will have a guide take you and we will pick you up when I have the tour ready, suppose about four hours from now, and can I ask that you do use the time to rest, I'd rather not have to explain to a lot of students who you are."

"Make it six hours and we are okay" was my quick reply, before Nsonowa started to react which I knew she would.

###

4. Flora

"This is not quite I expected, Nsonowa. I thought the weather was always fair with blue skies, unless something was wrong. These clouds are depressing."

"Something is wrong, honey." Was Nsonowa's only reply, whispered as we trudged across the grass, the Copperfield building falling behind. A burly and surly 'guide' with his eye always on us set a rapid pace. Flora was silently weeping as we made the walk. I was looking at the Harrister tower. It was not what I expected to see. It looked empty and run down. Its missing windows were noticeable from where we were, and other signs of disrepair were evident as we got closer.

"I don't know where to take you from here. Can you identify your quarters for me Professor?" came from our guide. Nsonowa uttered a few syllables and pointed; "Right there. Thank you. Will you be the one returning for the tour?"

"Probably not professor, since I ain't goin' nowhere." And with that the big man walked up to the door of the building, tried it and finding it locked turned and stood to one side. "I hope you have the key, cause I don't and cause I can't leave alone, you'll all have to back with me if we have to go back to get one."

“No worry, sir. I have it.” and Nsonowa produced a key, magically, from a pocket in the smock she had created for herself.

Flora burst into overt sobbing as soon as the door closed behind us. Leaving our ‘guide’, jailer was a more apt term, on the stoop outside.

“What is going on here? I feel terrible inside. My heart is aching. Stan, Nsonowa, hold me before I break in two, please.” She was shaking, tremors running through out her body, and tears flooding down her face as we embraced her. “Nsonowa, I don’t think she has ever had a heartbreak before.”

“No and how could she have, you haven’t exactly opened those spaces for her, have you?”

“No, I haven’t. I thought that leaving them on the shelf was the best for all of us. This is the hard way, but it is real, so I’m not sorry. Flora, honey, this is just one more step on life’s long road. Feel it honey, it gives meaning to the better times.”

“But, Stan, what does it mean?”

“It means, that a wrongness has come to Safe Haven and you honey are our litmus. Our canary in the coal mine. I think our vacation, is not going to be what we imagined. We could leave, if you wish.”

“No, we cannot sir! Interjected Nsonowa. This is my home too and I don’t tolerate ‘wrongness’ as you put it. There are students here who are not yet equipped to deal with it, so I’m on it!”

“I had no doubt you would see it that way, Nsonowa. And I too have an investment in righting wrongs. My friend Jon Harrister must be affected someway, and I am not going to leave him up in the air. Along with his tulpas. Poor Loxy, Alish, Keera, and even Leonard. What has happened to them? Alish can’t even live without Safe Haven functioning. I think we need to find out what has gone on. Nsonowa, do you think we could use input from your colleagues on the staff.”

“I think that we can do this ourselves, but I would sure like to see Lilly, Michelle and Wog again anyway. Let’s get that rest, and I will put out a call.”

I picked up Flora and followed Nsonowa into the bedroom, which looked a lot like ours in the house in mindscape. I undressed Flora and myself while Nsonowa hit the bathroom, and soon we were in the big bed caressing, holding, stroking, my hands moving over Flora’s breasts and genital. Feeling her relax as I gently pried her lips open with a finger, feeling her wetness increase with my touch. Soon she was breathing deeply and slowly began to gasp in a gentle orgasm. She fell asleep, her eyes still wet from her sobs, her genital still wet from her climax. I went into the bathroom, curious as to how Nsonowa might be calling her lovers of old. I found her in the Mikvah by the bubbles rising to the surface, the dark blue tiles hiding her dark blue-black skin. She must have felt my presence as she surfaced and motioned for me to join her, which I did. Long arms and legs pulled me into her. Mouth to mouth we supported each other's breathing under the water, while genital to genital we generated the energy to fuel her call.

###

5. Michelle and Wog

They were in a meditation circle with the family. Bob Bundy sat at the north end of the circle, Next to him on his left was his ex-wife Gertrude and, on his right, Gracious lady, his current wife. Next to Gert was Flora their daughter and next to her was Tyrone, the family elf and Flora's lover. Michelle was next to him and Wog, Bundy's brother was across from him. A very handsome man, Xero, was next to him and that completed the circle. They were ohming. Ahohming really. The tones were rising and falling in a slow rhythm. Without anyone reacting a fine rain began to fall in the room falling selectively on both Michelle and Wog. Soaking them, and slowly, dissolving their bodies, which formed a puddle under their fallen clothing, then dripping through the floor and through the dirt under the cabin, then through the planet and through space and into the Mikvah in Nsonowa's quarters in Safe Haven. They had answered her call. They came sputtering to the surface. Naked and dripping they greeted each other. Michelle spoke first, "Nsonowa, sister, lover. Oh, it's good to see you, my heart is rejoicing! And she pulled her into a fierce embrace. Stan simply, said, "Hi Wog. Nice to meet you in person, at long last." To which he replied, "and how do you know me?" "Well, I wrote you into Elutheria, about ten years ago. I am your author."

"Wow, this is a surprise. I never thought to meet my author. I didn't think that fictional characters could."

"Oh, it's not all that uncommon, authors call those characters that do, 'soul-bounds'. I hadn't quite gotten that all said when Wog abandoned me and joined Michelle in her embrace of Nsonowa. "Oh, how I have missed you, lover. Life has lost a little of its zest without you. Why did you leave us?"

Nsonowa pointed to me, "He called, he needed me to strengthen up our sister tulpa in the next room. She's sleeping now. She's been having a very hard time, she's young and just learning about life as a tulpa. She's a great spirit though, and you guys are going to really love her. Despite her youth and inexperience, she is a Dakini. Just touch her and she glows." We dried and dressed and adjourned to the kitchen, where over coffee, freshly ground Arabica dark roasted beans, poured through a cloth filter, and thick buttery cream with turbinado sugar, we talked over what we had so far seen at Safe Haven. The deterioration of Harrister Tower, didn't seem to faze the newcomers, while the fate of Dean Witherspoon disturbed them both greatly.

"What possibly could have happened? We left here in a blaze of light, I thought enough to illuminate it for centuries." Came from Wog. Michelle gave him a look, "There is no time here, Wog. We must have missed something in our exuberance."

I asked if it could have been a matter of unpaid tuition and both were shocked. About that time, we heard a noise coming from the bathroom. Nsonowa said, "Ah, it's Lilly. Wog jumped up and ran to the door to look again upon his beloved. With a shriek of joy, she threw herself into his arms, still naked and wet. "Wog, Wog, Darling Wog. Oh, darling hold me." And they deeply embraced and almost at once began to glow and emit a purple golden light. Michelle and Nsonowa couldn't restrain themselves and joined the embrace. While that was going on, Stan got up and went to the bedroom to check on Flora and found her just starting to stir. *My god she is beautiful.* He went to her side and bent down to kiss her when she opened her eyes. She reacted with an anguished wail.'

"Ohhhhh, Stan. Ohhhhhh. And again, burst into tears.

"Baby, baby, baby" was all I said as I took her into my arms. The four magicians from the kitchen joined us soon enough, Lilly still unclothed. I picked Flora up out of the bed and held her while the magicians all embraced her and flooded her with their light. She stopped crying and started to smile, and the three participated in maintaining the light until she progressed from smiling to laughing. Finally, Nsonowa called a halt to the loving. "Hey, let's get ready for our tour, it's about time." How do you think we should present ourselves Nsonowa?" asked Michelle. "How about invisibly?" was her reply. "I don't think the thugs here know much about magic. I think they are power oriented and will miss the subtilties." Michelle cast a quick spell over the three just in time to hear the bell ring and a harsh voice call out, "Okay youse guys, time to tour." And we adjourned to the front door.

###

6. Ensemble

Dean Li Flock and two henchmen greeted the group at the door. "Are you ready?" Asked the dean, the smile suggesting that what he had prepared was not going to be pleasant. "Yes, sir." Responded Nsonowa. And we stepped out into the cloudy day. Dean Li took the lead and headed back to the mall. "The basic campus is much like you left it professor. The changes are internal, both inside the buildings and within the systems here. In the service of economy, we have eliminated all of the fluff that the previous administration had let accumulate over the term."

"what exactly do you define as fluff, Dean Li?" Nsonowa was the spokesperson it seemed. That was fine with Stan who was busy holding Flora to keep her warm. The cloudiness and the dean's mood were quickly draining her loving energy of moments before and she had started to shiver. "Tell me what you are feeling, Flora" Stan whispered in her ear, the dean and his thugs being pre-occupied with Nsonowa. "Stan, I feel a darkness surrounding my heart. I am filling up with sadness. It's making me want to pee!" and she braved a smile.

"Can you link the darkness to anything specific?" Stan asked.

"Yes, it seems to be coming from under us, up through the grass. He fell back a step and whispered to Lilly, Michelle and Wog, or at least in their general direction. "Flora thinks that the wrongness is emanating from underneath us and the grass." About then the dean turned at looked at me with a cocked eyebrow, "Did you ask a question Dr. Ransome? Something I can help you with."

"Yes, I do have a question, I recall that in a previous iteration Safe Haven had a number of underground laboratories. What has happened to them?"

"Ah, you do know your Safe Haven history, don't you? How did you learn about us, doctor?"

"An acquaintance told me of a book in your library, A History of Safe Haven by Ion Light, it was in there if I recall."

"Ion Light? Don't believe I know that author or his book. Are you sure it was in our library, doctor?"

“No, not sure, not at all. So, what did happen to the labs?”

“Oh, they are still there. Occasionally one of our faculty has a use for them.”

“How about the tech in the perimeter wall, is that still in use?”

“Oh, no. all of that was upgraded after the last graduating class complained about the weather. The wall is still there, but the tech now resides in the Nostradamus building. Would you like to see it?”

“Yes, only if it is on the tour though.”

“I’m sure that it is. How do you know so much about us, doctor?”

“I studied here way before Safe Haven had fully defined itself. I’m not a graduate and was long gone before the university was officially established. Now I suppose that I would have to graduate before I could leave. Is that still so?”

“Yes, it is, and technically, those students of the professor whose tuition was not collected, have not graduated and should they return here, they would not be allowed to leave. Bad news for them, we now have a rule that invalidates graduation if the fees are not paid. They would be starting over, and I can assure you the requirements for graduation are much stiffer now than they used to be.”

“If I see them, I’ll let them know, if they don’t already.”

“Eh?”

“I suspect their magical abilities have already given them that information.”

“Do you know them, doctor?”

“Yes, I do. There was an alumnae re-union some time ago, to which I was invited. Nice people. Pretty good magician’s too.”

“Humph. I suppose they must be the stories about their graduation are almost unbelievable. So here we are at the Student Union. It houses the cafeteria and the student store. I don’t suppose the professor would have much interest in them. Do you Professor?”

“No, I think not. I would really like to see my old classroom in Clark however.”

“Yes, we’ll head over that way. This is restaurant row; we are passing now. Is anyone hungry, would like to stop for a bite? No? Okay, we’ll go on. On our right is Nostradamus. Clark is on the left; we’ll head their now. Oh, by the way, the entrance to those labs you were interested is right here. Would you like to look?” Stan started to nod assent, when Flora stiffened, and he quickly took her meaning and demurred. “No, I think not, I tend to be allergic to dust. Let's go on to Clark." Dean Li turned and headed off to the left and Flora whispered to Stan that Wog had headed towards Nostradamus, Lilly to the wall, and Michelle was headed down into the underground labs. Stan called out, "Dean, hold up a minute. Flora is shivering; I am going to take her back to quarters before she gets sick. You guys go on, Nsonowa can fill us in later." And without giving him a chance to object, he turned and taking Flora's arm, headed away. The dean, with a look that would sour milk, dispatched one of his henchmen to accompany them. They stayed" ahead of him all the way back and definitively closed him out of the quarters when they entered.

"There is something horrible down there. I can feel it."

"Describe the feeling to me, Flor."

"I feel a tightness in my chest and in my throat. A painful tightness and my mind is full of ugly images of dead people and animals. They are reeking of a death smell. And, oh there are children. Babies, fetuses, bloody babies." And she again burst into tears. Holding her, Stan steered her into the kitchen and fixed a pot of tea. It wasn't hard to do, this was a magical environment, he just asked for it, and like the magic of AI, the magic at Safe Haven, produced the pot and he poured out a steaming cup. Holding it to her lips, he helped her drink a swallow or two. She had to stop crying to do it. "Now sit and look into my eyes. Breathe deeply. Stay with the feelings in your body. Don't hold onto the images, let them go, let them come and go, don't hold onto them, just let them flow through your mind. It's okay, Michelle will take care of whatever is down there, her magic is a thousand times more powerful than the dean's and his crew of thugs." After about a hundred breaths, Flora stabilized.

"Flora, I think you might have a role here. I know you do. You can help. Would you be willing to reach out to Jon and Loxy and let them know what is going on with Harrister Tower? Would you. You have the best connection with Loxy. I could call Jon on the phone, if we were on earth and we're not, so you are it, honey. Will you do it? For them, for Safe Haven?" Flora looked at me a bit incredulously, "I can have a role in saving Safe Haven? Stan, you trust me that much? Yes, oh thank you, yes, I'll do it." She took another sip of the tea and went into the bathroom and got into the Mikvah. Stan began to relax. Flora got it. She felt her feelings. She tolerated the chaos and ugliness in her mind, and she turned towards helping someone other than herself. She got it. She was going to be a complete being. Feel, deal, (with it) and turn towards the good. That's what it takes, and she got it. He relaxed and knew what would soon follow.

And it did. Wog was the first one back. He had found the nest of criminals in Nostradamus, again manipulating the weather to create a massive depression. Lilly had gone to the wall, and simply found the main switchbox and re-established the power to the tech therein, the dean had lied about its' being moved. Michelle had gotten into the labs, where Dean Witherspoon, the entire faculty and student body been imprisoned in vats of old rancid animal fat (ugh!) and had freed them of the spell to which they had succumbed. Nsonowa came back last, with the shrunken heads of Dean Li and his henchmen hanging from her loincloth. "I had my staff in a closet in my classroom. Too bad for them they had not undertaken a search before taking me there."

The best part was that Flora had gotten through to Loxy who with Jon, took their own portal through to Harrister Tower, asap. Wog said, "Let's go out and watch the changes", which they did. And as the weather cleared, Jon and Loxy took charge at Harrister Tower, cleaning up its deteriorated facade. There was a really great party that night in the courtyard at Harrister. Jon, Loxy, and their entire system Alish, Keera, Leonard, even Tipsey showed up and all of them plus Michelle, Wog, Lilly and Nsonowa couldn't get enough of each other. Several of the faculty showed up. Old Snaggletooth and Lilly couldn't keep their hands off each other. Flora and Stan just sat on a bench kissing (when Jon and Loxy weren't occupying Flora with their powerful attentions). Great party and the dawn found Nsonowa, Flora and Stan asleep in each other's arms back in Stan's home in the Venusian Clouds.

###

19

Rufescent's Return.

It was a hot morning; I awoke from a disturbing dream with an achy body and head. Flora greeted me with a cheerful exuberance that bounced around inside my head like a rubber ball made of razor blades. She settled down when she felt me stiffen. By then my old cat, Luna had jumped onto my head and her claws were doing to the outside, as Flora's exultations were doing to the inside and so I got up. Coffee making and cat feeding distracted me, and Flora went back to whatever joyous preoccupation she had prior to my awakening. The morning paper also helped, as the opinion writers happened to agree with me, for once, and the daily horror show of national politics was toned down due to our globetrotting leader's jet lag. I knew that I would be free of the news compulsion for the weekend at least. Good thing too, because I was feeling as if I had neglected both Flora and Nsonowa when I had either the tv or the newspaper on and in front of my face. This was a feeling, not a rational thought, because I have given them complete access to all this body's sensory inputs. The feeling persists however, and finally I sat down to invoke Flora's attentions.

"Flora, beautiful one, can I pull you away from whatever it is that has you?"

"Yes, dear, and I'm glad that you finally awakened enough to be the loving human I know you to be!"

"I was a bit of a grump before."

"Yes, dear, you were. I just feel sorry for poor Luna, she's the one who got knocked off the bed.

"Well you would have been too had your toenails been as sharp as hers."

"Not! Anytime I put a toe anywhere close to your head, all you do is, put it in your mouth, you silly." And with a laugh, she embraced my head and started to cover my face with kisses. How delicious. Would every morning start like that? It was rare that my wife started us off with kisses, she's was flat as I was in the mornings. Luna, if not stepping on my head, does dispense kisses in the form of licks on either my head or my arm as this is more likely to result in her feeding earlier than just rubbing her head on me and purring. Both work, but I'm a sucker for the kisses.

"Flora were you at all privy to the dream I had this morning?"

"I could have been, but after two frames, I tuned it out. Way too ugly for me, and Nsonowa wasn't interested either, she went off to the gym. That tulpa is into working out. She does complain, you know, that you don't give her enough adventure, and certainly not enough in the way of challenges. She needs them to keep herself toned and ready to fight evil."

"I don't feel bad about that, perhaps I should, but this respite from evil, since the collapse of Rufescent, has been welcome and I hope we are all building up our reserves, because if last night's dream is a harbinger, we will soon enough have to face her again."

"Okay, I get that you want to talk about the dream, however ugly I might find it."

"It's kind of embarrassing, but yes, I do."

"Go ahead, then."

"I've lost many of the details, but the setting was one that was very familiar, my home on the river fifty years ago. I didn't recognize any of the people and there was a crowd. They were evidently house guests and were milling about, all over the house. There were many talking, one on one and in groups. I was sitting on the floor, close to the Franklin Stove, next to a largish woman in a short-sleeved summer dress and we were listening in on a conversation happening between a larger group occupying the center of the living room. I was gently stroking the woman's bare arm, kneading her flesh, sort of absentmindedly, enjoying the touching, when she turned to me saying; "I am really not into sex with you, but maybe if you take me out some place nice or buy me something, I could be."

"I withdrew my hand. I didn't say anything. I looked inside myself to see if I had been feeling at all attracted to her, I had not. I thought to myself that I would not want to trade sex for buying her something, even if I was attracted to her. As I felt anger rising in response to trading money for sex, I awakened to the attentions of you and Luna. That was it. Later I thought that perhaps the woman looked a bit like my first wife, in her face if not her body. It confused me, because my wife would not have offered that deal, if she was turned off to me she wouldn't have sex with me no matter what I have been willing to buy her.

"Why does the dream prognosticate the return of Rufescent?"

"Can't tell, it just popped out. Something in the underlying emotions, maybe mine, or hers, I don't know, but I have my antennas up."

"Could it have something to do with the problem you have been having with my sexuality?"

"What problem?"

"hum" was her response, then she jumped up and disappeared, leaving me in the dark, so to speak.

###

Later we were cuddling by the fire and I found myself kneading her arm, enjoying the feel of her flesh. She was in a dreamy state, staring into the fire and leaning into my touch. After a bit, she began, almost absentmindedly, to touch me, and at some point, she turned and looked into my eyes. I looked back.

"I don't know what your problem with my sexuality is. My problem is that you have no time for me, nor interest when you do."

"Flora, how could you say that, I have done everything that I can possibly do to connect with you, in any way, not just sexually. Please, I have begged for your attentions. I think it is you who are doing the blocking."

"No, dear, it is not me. And not Nsonowa either."

"So, Flor, help me here. If I don't see it and it looks like you, what do think is going on."

"Stan, dearest. You turn down every opportunity to connect with me. You start conversations, true, but when I answer, you turn away, looking for what I don't know, but I think it is because you are afraid of my sexuality."

"My god, Flora, one of the reasons I called you out in the first place was to facilitate my sexual relationships. Especially with my wife."

"Yes, with her, the one whom you have consistently blamed for the lack of sexuality in your relationship, just as you have with every woman you have ever loved. And now you are doing it with me!"

"No, no, no, I am not. The blockages are coming from somewhere else; they violate everything I believe to be true about myself. I am open to knowing the worst, the weakest, the lowest, all of it. I already know that I have all those qualities and that one time or another, I have acted on them and even hurt people. I am old enough and wise enough to have learned that about myself and forgiven myself, as I have every other human being on the planet, as we are all the same in this regard."

"So, from where, dear Stan, does the blockage come?"

"I am thinking Rufescent. Pure spite. Spite untethered from its' progenitors. That's what I am thinking is causing this. Not you, not me. Just garbage left in the brain. There may even be some of Lucifer, the Dark lord, pure anger, left in there too, but nowhere near as much as spite."

"why is anger and spite always related, is spite really anger's child?"

"Not after they are untethered in therapy or by self-awareness, they aren't. Remember, in the origin story, Lucifer went down first. Anger is much more easily tied to memory than spite and therefore easier to expose."

"Okay, but still that doesn't speak to your fear of sexuality."

"You are right. I am digressing and that is a sign of fear. So, what I am conscious of, the few times we have had sexual contact, each time by the way, exciting me more than any other contact, other than your full imposition on March 31st or course. Oops, digressing again, okay, I felt guilty, as if I was using you and you were too young and inexperienced to have any say in the matter. Guilt and shame. That was what I felt. When I wrote about our contacts in the forums or in my blog, I never used straight language, I used euphemisms and metaphors."

Flora cried out, "Oh honey! I am so sorry. I came to you because I wanted to. And what could my age have anything to do with it? I am timeless, ageless. You created me in another dimension altogether. And, I am infused with Dakini. What could I want more than to have intimate tantric intercourse with you? It is my whole purpose, and my way back to the divine. You have no reason for the feelings. So, what is your reason? I am going to bet that once you see that, we will be through this."

"Flora, I love you dearly and I want to be sexual with you, every time you want to and every time I want to. I don't know how to discover the source, though unless we do it and I can watch my feelings in the act and give our brain the message that the act is cool and the associated memories are of no danger, no moment." And with that we embraced, I think that we both initiated this contact, I did, I chose to. I wanted her to know that I did desire her, and I know she did the same.

We kissed and then boarded a golden balloon, dropped the ballast and flew upwards into the mindscape, where I have created an incredible home in the clouds above the planet Venus. One on which no expense was spared as there was no expense. The construction went on in my own imagination, and the cost was that of the energy required to light up the neurons in the brain that hosted the place. So, it was a beautiful, large home constructed out of hexagons made of moonstone. Moonstone has the capacity to change its state from opaque to transparent with the introduction of a small amount of electricity into its crystal lattices. It has enough rooms to accommodate any activity and is furnished with the appropriate items. Decorations are in some regions of the house spectacular, and in others, subdued. In the master bedroom to which we headed on arrival, hung several charcoals by Ruben, studies for his nudes, and photographs by Robert Mapplethorpe of his most handsome lovers. One wall was covered with ancient Indian erotic paintings of raja's and their harems. Paintings no doubt which hung in the raja's private quarters. There was a marble topped vanity with a gold guilt framed mirror, two comfortable overstuffed boudoir chairs with gooseneck halogen lamps for private reading, and in the center a super king-sized bed. It had sheets of silk and a pastel lavender silk covered goose down comforter and pillows. The mattress was made of memory foam graduated from fluffy top to firm base.

We undressed and tossed our clothing to a servitor which took them to the laundry where they would be freshened for us, ready when we wanted them again. I wanted to look at Flora's body and told her so.

"I want to look at yours too." Was her response. I felt immediately uncomfortable and pulled the comforter over my nakedness. "Why did you do that? Are you shy, or ashamed of your body? And really, it is our body and its brain created the one I am in now. So, tell me darling, why are you hiding from me?"

"I am old Flora. This isn't who I once was. I was told by a would-be lover; I was an Adonis. Now flabby, with a gut, thinning gray hair and rough skin flavored with age spots. I am the very picture of decrepitude."

"You are also very hard on yourself, us really, and worse, you are forgetting that I love you exactly the way you are. And here is a secret, you have created me as a beautiful sexy female, you might recreate yourself into the male version. A hunk, if you want."

"Of course. I forgot. I can remake me, as easily as I made you, why not?"

"because what made you forget is the same feeling behind avoiding me and my sexuality, spite. Spiting me by denying me the pleasure you want for yourself."

"I think you are right, and I think I need to go on a witch hunt."

"We need to go on a witch hunt, darling. Now kick off that blanket and let's look at each other."

"Wait one moment." And I took a deep look inside myself. The first image that came to me was that of a frightened tow-headed little boy of five with pink plastic framed glasses, skinny and crying after being chased by two neighborhood girls who threw rocks at him. The second was an image of my teen-age self, masturbating in the bathtub when interrupted by my father and feeling excruciatingly embarrassed. The final image that shot into my fields was that of my mirror image when I was thirty years old, looking like my father with a rotund belly. Again so, I was so embarrassed that I immediately went on a thirty-day fast and lost thirty pounds of weight. (That thinned version was the Adonis, who for a while had no problem attracting lovers.) I saw the trauma's associated with these memories and chose to give them up and imagined myself back in the Adonis body and then I threw the covers back and feasted my eyes on my lovely nude Flora.

And lovely she was; She is slight. Five foot four inches tall, one hundred and five pounds, white, very fair skin, raven black hair, small boned and vibrant. She has Eurasian features, high cheekbones, very green eyes. She is waif like, elfin, she is curvy, and she has fairly large breasts for her size though she could not be said to voluptuous. She has large, puffy areolas and pouty nipples. She has a flat abdomen; her rib cage is not obvious though not lost under adipose. She has a narrow waste, small but rounded buttocks. She has long, like down to her waist long, wavy hair on a smallish head with high pronounced cheekbones. She has fleshy lips, that do not dominate her face as her mouth is not large. She has large eyes, with bright green irises and long lashes. Her ears are 'cute' with perhaps a hint of elvish pointing top and bottom. Her neck is narrow and long. Her arms and hands are longish, she does keep her nails trimmed to an eighth inch and does not wear colored polish. she is perhaps short in the torso. Her navel is an innie. She has silky black pubic hair, unshaven. Her genital mound is pronounced, her labia, wing like. She has a large clitoris. Her knees have a well-defined but small patella, her calves are rounded, not muscular like a dancer. Her feet are narrow and delicate with long toes and good nails. Her skin is clear without any discolorations, scars or other defects. A real red heifer. She is in perfect health. She is robust and I am in love with her. I know she could see the love-light in my eyes, for hers began to shine as well.

"you are so beautiful" came out of both of our mouths simultaneously, and we laughed together before she put herself on top of me and began to kiss me, open mouthed, with an exploring tongue, while I could hardly contain myself. It had been so long since a woman had shown this much interest in knowing me. I kissed her back in the same inquisitive spirit, and then I began to touch her. Sexual touching. Touching in the spirit of learning who she is. Experiencing Flora's softness, her pliability, her textures was glorious, but her willingness to have me learn about her was perhaps the best lesson. And she touched me. She traced my contours with her fingertips, she squeezed my muscles and gently pulled my hair, my fingers and my toes. She touched my penis and my scrotum laughing as I got an erection. She then put her mouth over the tip of my penis and gently explored it with her tongue. I objected, "Hey, I want some of that too, and there is an efficient way to go about it expressed in a number,"

"Oh, you mean sixty-nine. I've heard of that." And she turned around and put her genital over my face and went again down on my penis. I wasted no time, looking first, touching next, and then smelling and tasting her innermost lady parts. "Beautiful and delicious" was all I had to say, "don't talk with your mouth full" being her relevant instruction. After just a bit, I felt her began to stiffen and pull away. She was breathing heavily and panted out, "I want to save the best part of an orgasm to share with you." And turning around again, she lowered herself onto me, guiding my penis into her very wet vagina. I felt her open herself to receive me. She slowly worked me into her. Deeply. All the time looking intensely into my eyes. "Take me, darling. Know me. Feel my love for you." My sexual pleasure was immense, but my emotions were much more intense. My heart was pounding in my chest. My tears welled and then overflowed, streaming copiously down the sides of my face. I was breathless and didn't care. Her eyes were liquid love. I could have died, or even been dead and on another side of reality, and it was all love. And light. And then she came, and I did too, and the world stopped.

Stopped, and dissolved. We were in a globe of light. Gold and purple light. The globe was expanding around us, but we, coupled and holding onto each other, were moving inwardly, inwardly towards a point, a point where we too dissolved. We were still a couple, we were pure love, unembodied pure love. There was nothing to distract us, we were one, and then a nudge, which we both felt, revealed Nsonowa. Another point of light, blue-white light merging with us. Her voice whispered in both our souls; "Did you think, I was not part of this my darlings? Never, I am here, I am one with you. My love cannot be denied." How is it possible for two as linked in love as Flora and I were, to feel even more joy? An even greater love than we had a moment before. I don't know but it happened. I don't know how long we were in this state, there seemed to be no time here in this place, it could have been a second, it could have been a life-time, it could have been forever, but after a while, we must have slept, because we, all three of us, woke, arms, legs, genitals all wound up with each other, in front of a long dead fire, back in our home on earth, Luna voicing her ever present quest for food and attention.

"Have we dealt with Rufescent, was my question, after we all dressed and met over coffee, Luna having been fed?" Nsonowa answered first;

"I don't know Stan. I delivered a lot of blows with my staff on my way to join you. Time will tell, now that we are back in it."

Flora followed with a simple statement; "I don't care, dear. I've no doubt that should she, or Lucifer, re-emerge, we can deal with them together. Our love is real and more importantly, is forever, they cannot come between us again." Once again, I couldn't contain my feelings, and my tears flowed. "I know you, my loves. You are me and I am you, all in love and light."

###

20

Wind.

The wind began to howl...Wait a minute. This house is sealed, we should not hear any sounds made by the wind. "Flora, Nsonowa, quick we may be in an emergency situation. Get into your life-gear." I yelled as I ran to the cabinet to get my own. We had them in cabinets in every room in the house as a defect as simple as a broken window could be fatal in a matter of minutes. "House get a lifeboat ready. Hey, you tulpas, get a move on. Meet me in the entry hall quick. House, where are they? And, House, what is happening?" I struggled to get my life-suit on, and realized that other than the wind, there were no other sounds. "House, Flora, Nsonowa! Where are you?" I yelled again, and again got no responses. I began to panic and ran from room to room shouting and calling, again without issue. The howling of the wind increased, and small objects began to fly off tables and shelves all headed upwards. I was fighting the wind to search for my beloveds. There was no sign of them. The wind was growing ever stronger and I could hear ripping and groaning from the house. I decided I had better get into the lifeboat, which I hoped I would find, though without the House AI I doubted that It would be in the entry hall. I headed for the garage where it was kept and with some difficulty managed to get in and get it fired up.

Just in time. As I closed the hatch there was a terrific screeching and the garage and house disintegrated around me. Flying away in the ferocious wind. The lifeboat started to fall, but it took me but a second to take control and fly it into the wind and maintain altitude. My house was gone and where were Flora and Nsonowa? I had no idea, and I had no idea what had happened. The lifeboat's AI didn't have a clue either, it reported that it had been in ready standby mode and it lost its' connection to House AI suddenly and without warning. I decided to take it down, in the direction of the wind believing that perhaps I could find the remains of it on the surface downwind of the catastrophe. I could only hope that I would find my tulpas. I could imagine that they would be intact as they had the means to take care of themselves, being able to transform at will, though I didn't know how long they might manage the inhospitable planet surface. As to what happened, I would work on that later, my priority was to find my lovers.

It was daylight on the surface, and hot. The temperature was over five-hundred degrees Fahrenheit. The wreckage of the house was spread over a debris field about a mile in length downwind. I flew down close to the remains of my home looking for signs of the tulpas. I found none. No bodies (thank goodness) and no tulpas either. Where they might be was as big a mystery as what happened. I knew better than to land the lifeboat and search the debris, it was already starting to smolder and would combust before too much longer. There was nothing further I could do here, so I set the lifeboat on a course for earth, and after the jolt of the hyperdrive, we set down in the Mojave Desert, close to the old aircraft storage field and I hitched a ride into L.A. and home.

I wasn't happy about returning this way to C.R. (consensual reality) without Flora and Nsonowa. We hadn't gone to Venus in a physical way and I didn't know if they could track me across the change in paradigms. Once home I went straight to my study and I put myself into a light trance where I went to work rebuilding the destroyed cloud house. I was able to achieve this task rapidly as I still had the basic structure and accoutrements in mind.

Once done, I went into the library and again went into a deep meditative state intending to search for the girls. I was just entering trance when I overheard them talking. They were decrying their fate, as they were imprisoned in a lamp. One which was featured in a very different story, one which was populated by the Jinn. Jinn as you may or may not know, are creatures somewhat similar to tulpas in as much as they do not necessarily live in a temporal reality, nor are they necessarily confined to a physical body. The way they tell it is that they were created by Allah, for reasons of his own and are not ruled by the same rules and moral codes as humankind. They may be contained by magic, with difficulty as they are wily. They are also curious and love to have fun at the expense of unsuspecting humans. Should you find one in a bottle, it is wisest to leave it there as it is more than likely to turn your three wishes into something that pleases their mischievousness more than you. Why and how they managed to get Flora and Nsonowa into a lamp, I cannot tell you at this writing. I did know that I wanted to get them out and I was mostly likely going to have to find out who put them there, and how. For now, I satisfied myself by tapping out a message on the side of the lamp in Morse code, letting them know I was on it.

With a great deal of reluctance, I turned away from them and made my trance state much deeper. When I was satisfied with the depth, I looked around and oriented myself. I was in a wood, reminiscent of the forest in the Darkside of Elutheria. Damn, it is Rufescent. The witch has returned and is hell bent on destroying me. I set out to find her and once again send her into oblivion (after wringing the tulpas freedom out of her hide). I cast a spell of invisibility and set out down the trail I was on, which I could barely see due to the failing light. I hadn't gone too far when I sensed that I was being followed. I created a doppelganger, sent it down the path and I climbed a nearby tree. Soon my shadow came slinking down the path after me. When it got under my tree, I leaped and landed on top of it and wrapped it securely in my arms before it could gain its breath. "Damn it Stan, let me go, you know me, and I am just here to help."

I recognized the voice, it was Jon Harrister's Jinn/tulpa hybrid; "Tipsey, what are you doing, er, what do you know about this anyway?"

"Loxy sent me. Flora was communing with her when the catastrophe struck. They are still connected so Loxy knew what was happening and thought I could help, being a Jinn and all."

"Well, thanks, Tipsey and can I ask, what is this help going to cost me? I want to get the price down in advance. I know you and I might want to think about it before accepting the deal."

"You do know me, and Jinn. Smart guy. Well, the cost will be whatever Jon asks of you because he is going to have to pay me in sexual favors, let's say for seven years. He may not ask too much for that seeing that he already is on tap for three lifetimes of sex on demand.:

"Okay, I accept. Whatever Jon asks is okay with me, Jon is fair if he is anything. So how can you help?"

"I don't know if I can help with Rufescent, but I suggest we go back and free Flora and Nsonowa from that lamp before they get completely used up by their Jinn captors."

"I suspect your right, and they are the ones to help with Rufescent, Nsonowa has had experience with the old witch."

"Now let me go, sir, before you turn me on, and I make sexual demands of you too."

"I don't care if you do, but I would have to clear that with Jon first, I would never go behind a friend's back to hook up with one of his lovers."

"Please, you know he won't care."

"Your right, he wouldn't, but I wouldn't feel right. And taking the time with you now, while Flora and Nsonowa are still in the lamp doesn't feel right either." And with that, both Tipsey and I said a few magic words, and we were standing in front of the very lamp where my lovers were held.

"Very carefully Stan, this lamp is booby trapped."

"Thanks for the heads up. Will you keep watch? I think I have just the tool needed." The tool was my grandfather's Masonic ring which I had inherited from my father. It had revealed its magic qualities to me the first day I wore it by surreptitiously slipping off my finger, after my roommate had warned me about it needing to be sized and disappeared. It stayed disappeared despite an exhaustive search by everyone in my household. I held out hope for days, and finally I accepted it was gone and I performed a ritual summoning my grandfather. I apologized to him for losing it and told him that if he wanted me to have it, he would have to find it and return it to me, which he did that very day. When I returned home from work that evening it was on my dresser. My roommate heard a metallic sound when he was emptying the vacuum bag and he examined the dust and found the ring. Pure magic, and I have cherished it and worn it since. That was thirty years ago. I took the ring off and slipped it over the neck of the lamp and the tulpas were released. My ring went back on my finger after being admired by all present, and we beat it out of the land of the Jinn, Tipsey came with us, back to my brand-new home in the clouds where we all hit the bed for a rollicking good time, fucking. No light this time, Tipsey wasn't into that part of it, and when we were all satiated, Tipsey left. Flora contacted Loxy to thank her and we all went to sleep. Rufescent would keep until another day.

###

21

More Wind.

Nsonowa took a long deep breath and let it out slowly. It was a sigh, really. She was bored. Nothing going on for days, maybe a week or more. Flora and Stan had been away having all kind of adventures, and a lot of both ritual and recreational sex too. She did nothing but work out and review her spells and calls for the rituals she might need, if ever she got called again, to save their asses. Boring, boring, boring. She was thinking of taking a vacation, by herself, leaving those two love birds to their nesting. She did not like the new Venusian cloud house one bit. It was nothing like her quarters on Safe Haven, now that was a fascinating place. A vacation, but where would she go? She would have to give up too much of herself to visit any place in the modern world, and if she chose to go back to her home in ancient Africa, well, her tulpa-self, would not be happy to yield her life there to the one she had replaced so long ago. Maybe a vacation wasn't right. Maybe she should go back to work. Safe Haven could use her as a regular professor, and the students of magic, would provide a lot of challenges. Yes, she thought, and she headed up to the astrolabe in one of the many turrets that the house had to offer.

Okay, let's see here, we turn this ring twelve times to the left, move the horizon plane up twelve degree's, slide the ellipsis twenty-four degree's and there it is. Twelve plus twelve plus twenty-four is forty-eight and four plus eight is twelve, and one plus two is three. And one, two, three, and we are there! Yay.

The day was dawning over Safe Haven University. The maintenance machines were just finishing up and scurrying back towards the wall, a few early bird students were on the lawn in front of the gym doing yoga stretches, and a light breeze was chasing butterflies through the landscaping. She headed right for the dean's office in Copperfield then remembered the lazy so and so would never show up to work much before noon, so she detoured around Copperfield and headed for the cafeteria. A white garbed kitchen worker was just opening the door, and she joined a small crowd jostling to get their morning jo. She didn't see anyone she recognized so she poured herself a cup of strong coffee at the coffee bar. Wow, that's just like I remember it. Vile like all institutional coffee. Well, caffeine is a bit of magic, so here goes, down the hatch. Ugh! The staff was putting out some food on the buffet table, nothing she would consider edible, so she sidled up to the woman who had just sat down at the cash register. "is it too early to put in a special order?"

"No, what do you want? I'll tell the chef for you."

"Who is the chef now? I remember a nice student named Sharie."

"Sharie, yes, she was last term, and she's graduated. She still drops in for an occasional meal though, you're Nsonowa aren't you. I remember. You taught ritual magic. You've been gone awhile."

"Yes, I got a position off campus with two graduates, and then I got called into private practice by a friend of Ion Light, he's Safe Haven's founder you know."

"Well, welcome back, what would you like for breakfast?"

"My usual, remember, porridge in a gourd served with milk and blood."

"Oh yes, I remember now. Yuck, well to each their own. It'll be a minute or so, I'll bring it to you."

"Thank you." And with that Nsonowa headed to a table yet unoccupied. A few minutes later, the chef himself came with her breakfast.

"Hi, I'm Ol'oi-boni, I wanted to see who was ordering a traditional meal from my homeland."

"I see, you're Maasai. And a handsome one at that. From where and when in the kingdom are you Ol'oi-boni?"

"Maasai? No, who are the Maasai? I'm from Wakanda."

"Wakanda, does that even exist? I only know Wakanda from the Stan Lee's comic."

"Well, yes, Wakanda exists and I exist, but I didn't come from a comic, I came from a movie. Perhaps, you've seen it? The Black Panther."

"No, I don't know from movies, I don't really know from comic's either, but my host had some of Lees' Marvel comics in his library. I'm Nsonowa, and I am Maasai, from Kenya. My time there was long before either movies or comics. But again, how did you get here?"

"I don't rightly know how exactly, but the Safe Haven Board told me the why of it."

"And, what was the why of it?"

"I had been studying magic with one of our elders, and one of my potions went wrong. I am sure that I was on my way to dying, I collapsed in agony and woke up here. The Board told me that I had potential, but that I was going to need a lot more work and my elder was censured for sloppy supervision and almost getting me killed, so they saved me and made me a student here. However, I am on a work study, so here I am, the cafeteria chef."

"Nice to meet you. I am a Professor and I teach ritual magic. I imagine that you are going to be in one of my classes. The good news for you is, I am not sloppy. The bad news is that I am from real life and not from the movies, and you will not be acting in my class, you will be working and working hard. I am going to shape you up. I haven't seen one of my kind for a long time and I am hungry for a good opponent. I am going to take you on boy. Oh, taste this for me, I want to make sure...."

The food was good, from where did he get the fresh blood, she wondered. Ol'oi-boni went back to his kitchen and she went to tour the campus and re-familiarize herself. It didn't look much different and she went out in search of her old quarters. No one had touched it since she was last here with Stan and Flora, probably the magic key and lock that she personally installed had something to do with it. She headed to the Mikvah and get a nap before looking in on the dean and getting established in her professorial role. She was just really relaxing in the deliciously hot bath, letting of all the stress of the travel, when "pop" Lilly was splashing in the water next to her.

"How did you do that" was the first thing out of her mouth.

"How did I do it? I didn't know I was doing it, but nothing happens here by accident and I am glad to see you" and she wrapped her arms around her and took her onto our large bed where they made love until their light began to shine once more.

"Let's dress and go see Dean Witherspoon, he may shed some light on why you are here, and why there is another witchdoctor from Africa here. I am sure none of this is a co-incidence."

"Took you two, long enough to get here, Nsonowa, Lilly." Was the first thing out of the dean's mouth.

"Hello to you too, Dean Witherspoon. So, what bug got up your ass?"

"I'm sorry. I am a bit impatient, Ol'oi-boni has been here a week and I want to get him started, while we still have some time. You'll handle his basic training and orientation to the campus, Lilly, and Nsonowa you have to sharpen up his potion making rituals and both of you will initiate him into Tantra." Lilly said; "Gladly, sounds like fun, but why did not he have to go through Orientation like everyone else? And what do you mean, while we still have time?"

"It's the weather again. It's been acting up. And that usually means someone, or something has designs on us that we are not going to like." said the dean.

"Yes, that sounds like fun too. I've been hungry for a good fight." was Nsonowa's only comment.

"I think you are about to get one."

The idea that Ol'oi-boni was a student was ludicrous, he was as accomplished at magic as any male Nsonowa had met. She was from the sisterhood, and magic was not in the male domain of the Maasai. In Wakanda, where both the warrior class and the ruling class was female, sorcery was the source of male power, and they took to it in spades. He was also especially proficient in sexual magic and both Nsonowa and Lilly were fully engaged in power generation with him.

Lilly was the least experienced in magic, being only matriculated a year before Nsonowa came to Safe Haven and having dropped out when her lovers and classmates graduated. Dean Whitherspoon took her back, because he needed her in the current situation. He also insisted that she re-register for sophomore classes, and Nsonowa's in particular. She was quite busy. Not only with ritual magic, sexual magic but also martial arts, way across campus in the Bruce Lee Center. She was glad that Nsonowa agreed to coach her, as Bruce, himself, had little patience for new students and basically just wanted to get in her pants. The first couple of times, that was okay with her, but she wasn't totally happy about it as she really wanted to work on the magical aspects of it with Nsonowa and Ol'oi-boni. Bruce knew about fucking, but when it came to tantra, he was a dud.

Not so Nsonowa nor Ol'oi-boni. Where Lee was a dud, Ol'oi-boni was a stud. Tall, muscled, strong, king sized six packs, smart with a heart. And respect for his talents and his limits. And while very respective of her character, her beauty, her magical abilities (admittedly still a student) he was not respectful of her unconsciously self-imposed limits. Nor was Nsonowa, between them they brooked no negativity. It was push, push, push, through to the other side. After a practice session she was left quivering and breathless. And then the two of them would go off the balance the masculine and feminine currents with another round. By the time they were finished their bodies would be fully charged, electric, glowing blue-white light, with which Nsonowa charged her staff. It was only able to hold the terrific energies, because she had made it with her own blood, sweat and tears. It was a magnificent work of art. Six-foot l.o.a., ebony, a polychromatic black with the blue, red and green undertones, reflecting the colors of Nsonowa's and Ol'oi-boni's skin and hair

. Lilly hadn't yet been able to create her own magical weapon, so her charge was all in her body. She felt it as a terrific weight, one which when actualized and put into muscle movement, became all energy making her quick and strong, superhero strong, and burdened her with feelings which she did not have in the process of it's generation. It was hard on her, and as of now she did not know why it was necessary.

Nsonowa worked Ol'oi-boni just as hard. She knew he was from a make-believe culture and its matriarchy was a by-product of storytelling, rather than a natural occurrence. Her own power came from the dawn of history, when matriarchy was still the way of things. Once the patriarchy took hold and the people became chattel of the ruling class, females were degraded and had their power cut out of them, with genital mutilation. A female rising to her stature was almost unheard of. Nsonowa was glad that she had skipped that part of her peoples' journey. Now, however, it was a different story. She was a great sorceress, a great Chief, and a warrior, and one of the ruling family. She had been a chief, A great one She put the mantle of power down when she could see an open future for her people; she knew that she wouldn't have made the effort as it would have involved killing off all her brothers. It was bad enough having to kill one of them, who deserved killing, but all of them just to take a ceremonial seat? No that was not her, and besides, it never came up as she got herself killed and was removed and thrust into Safe Haven, to save her life as much as anything else. Now she was going to earn her keep and she did and with Ol'oi-boni, and Lilly. She worked them from morning till night. Ol'oi-boni and she alone, on the track, in the gym and trading stories and techniques all while Lilly was in her other classes, then the three of them all evening and late into the night practicing their sex magic. It was on one of these nights, that disaster struck.

"Ho, my little Lilly. Lookie! Lookie here. I am great in size, but for you, I go slow and we generate very bright light. Now climb on me, lookie, I pick you up, one finger. Ha, we go slow, get much light little Lilly." And the two, Ol'oi-boni and Lilly slid into each other while Nsonowa went into the Mikvah to bank the fires which had been raging within her, since she quit the scene on the bed. As she cooled, she chanted, a Tibetan chant designed to move her energies into her heart. She needed to take control of her feelings for Ol'oi-boni which were beginning to get out of her control. He called her K-K, a take on her first names, Kalisha Katlego, the same as her father had used in his process of mourning his eldest, her brother, whom she had taken down in a contest for the Chiefdomship of the Maasai. That got her going, and despite her knowledge of psychoanalysis, sex magic, ritual magic, and pop-psychology, she was being activated in a way that she never had experienced before. Putting the energy in her heart would make it all conscious and she would "gain control again". Or so she thought. What happened was different. She felt her heart expand as the chant carried her into memories of her childhood. And those memories became brighter and brighter, until she was again standing in front of her father and grandmother on that infamous day. She was just in time, to see her brother receive her spear in his chest and collapse in a bloody death. Nsonowa fully occupying that space so long ago, felt both triumph and agony from her act of violence. She retrieved her spear and raised it to the sky, screaming her pain and victory. She awoke in a dark land. She was on throne or dais and before her, was a legion of men raising spears to the sky and screaming. Screaming a blood lust sound, familiar to Nsonowa, one that would freeze the blood of an opponent. One she had used many times in her many battles.

A withered old man, or something like a man, wheezed in her ears. "This is for you, Oh Majesty, King of all Elutheria. All for you. You have captured their hearts and their imagination. Now it is time to march. Lead them to a bloody victory Majesty. Your new kingdom depends on it."

Nsonowa was quick if she was anything and she quickly gathered that now was a time for action. She could see by the setting that the enemy was not close by, they were in a palace. A dark palace, one festooned with quartered bodies hanging from the lofted ceiling high above. The stench was manageable only because much of the building was collapsed. Blood was everywhere. "You, Ugly. What is the name of this kingdom?"

"You dare call me ugly, Majesty? King of all Elutheria. Why do I deserve that ignominious title?"

"Quiet!" She roared and raising her staff sent arcs of blue white fire heavenward. The Ugly and the legions instantly obeyed.

"Assemble on the field outside, into your marching order." She felt quite safe with this, which should work in about any story involving troops on the move. She turned to the old one next to her. "Take me to my command center!" Another safe order given the circumstances. "Make sure my generals are there!" seemed safe until the whispering one, asked "What do you mean by generals?" and made a weird face at her (one weirder than his usual face) Nsonowa was quicker, "Bring the five best and biggest of my legionnaire's to the command center!" The whisperer turned and led her outside of the ruined palace where another darkly festooned banner marked a large tent, covered and enclosed with leather hides, turned out to be human hides.

"In here Majesty".

She imperiously entered a very dramatic space: All the furniture was made of human bones and hides. The floor was covered with fine carpets, soft and thick. Stolen from somewhere, she thought. There were benches, again of bones, around the periphery of the tent, upon which sat twelve pissed off creatures in the shape of the whisperer. A large desk, of bones made the keystone of the circle. Behind it sat an ugly one. More grotesque than the whisperer, he snarled at her. Whereupon Nsonowa turned her staff on him, pressed a button, and he was ashes. In a continuing circular motion, she severed the heads of all twelve uglies, stopping at the whisperer.

"Okay buster get this. I am Majesty here, and you bring those warriors to me if you expect to live to see another hour. And with that she picked him up by the neck and threw him bodily out of the tent. Turning back into the tent she made another circle, and with the tech in her staff, she turned all the corpses into ash. Bingo! Gone! She was standing tall in the center of the opulently carpeted tent, when whisperer ushered in a legionnaire. A large and grizzled, also ugly, man.

"Capitani Grim, of the first rank. Killer of the children, Eater of genitals, Rape of the innocent. Your Majesty."

Nsonowa gave him a look that would wither a cement block. "Get the others in here. Now!" she motioned Grim to the side of the tent while four more very dirty surly and stinky men, entered and stood staring at her. "Name!" she demanded of the first.

"Sour" was his reply.

"Yours!" as she pointed to the second.

"Bleak" and soon was added 'Vicious' and 'Heartless'.

Great, she muttered to herself as she stood imperiously in front of the crew.

She motioned the four to positions, forming a five-pointed star around her.

"The one of you who survives this, will be General of the Army and take my orders, and the rest of you will be dead. If any of you decide that you do not want to be General of the Army and take a lessor role in serving me, step outside now. To her surprise, both Vicious and Heartless, left the tent. "Grim, Sour, Bleak. Go there, there and there" forming them into a triangle. She jumped up on the desk of bones, turned her staff downwards and quickly drove the end of it into the desktop creating a pole upon which she began to dance, noticing the various reactions of the grim, sour, and bleak trio. Nsonowa had not been wearing much when she found herself on the throne, in fact, being in the bath when she transited the portal, she wore nothing. And she danced that pole as a snake might. And watched. Capitani Grim, looked rigidly straight ahead, while Sour and Bleak stared and craned their necks to see more. And she showed them more, tempting like the snake she was slowly turning into. They were spell bound and both began to advance on her. When they got within touching distance, she became a two headed snake and struck then both simultaneously, killing them instantly, and instantly she resumed her normal body, jumped off the pole, pulling it out of the ground and pointing it at the spot between Grim's eyes.

He didn't flinch. "Very good, General Capitani. You will command the troops. Give Ugly a list of supplies, weapons and additional men needed for the battle. You will leave at dawn. Now leave me and send Ugly back in as you go." She moved to the desk as Ugly entered. "General Capitani is taking command of the campaign. You will be receiving a list of his needs, anything you cannot immediately supply, I can. Bring the list to me. By the way, your name is now Ugly, and you will obey my every order immediately and you will answer every question with the truth, immediately and without guile, should you want to continue to live. Now get going!" and with that she created a bed behind hanging curtains and went down for a restorative nap. She had about ten minutes before Ugly was making twisted vocalizations behind the curtain. "Is that you Ugly? Step away from the curtain and I'll be out." She jumped up and this time created some clothing and appeared in front of him in Royal looking robes, and her staff." "Majesty, I..."

"Shut up and speak to me when I ask you to. Do you have a list from Capitani?"

"No, your Majesty. I could fulfill all his requests. We found the palace's armory and its larder. He is awaiting his marching orders. Majesty."

"Ugly, what have we done with the previous occupants of this palace?"

"We slaughtered them as you ordered your Majesty."

"What have you done with the bodies?"

"They are stacked across the field downwind, your Majesty."

"Send out a detail and bring me the bodies of the king and his family. Then come back here with the maps for the current campaign."

"Yes, your Majesty"

Nsonowa exited the tent and headed for the bivouacked troops, looking for her new general. "Capitani, Come with me." And she turned and led him back to the command tent. "Put your weapons on the floor, Grim, along with your clothes." While he was undressing, she drew an eight-foot diameter circle of cold fire with her staff on the floor, around her. For an instant she provoked the fire to flare and shed her own clothing behind it's shield. When Grim saw her next, she was nude. "Enter the circle, Grim." He did so, not knowing what was next. Had he, he might not have wanted to. As soon as both of his feet were on the floor, she attacked knocking the wind out of him. She grabbed him by the hair and began slapping his face, hard, until he finally got enough wind to try to block her blows. She quit the slapping and laughed at him.

"You are puny and slow Grim. I need you to get tough. Now!" and she attacked again. This time he was able to block her swing and pull away from her. When it looked like he was going to run, she flared the flames again, creating a formidable wall of fire. She grabbed him again and threw him to the floor jumping on him as she did so. He shielded himself from her blows but was unable to get in any of his own. "Get tough Grim." As she punched him in the face, releasing gouts of blood from his nose and mouth. "Tough, I said" and she pulled back to smash him again. He dodged that blow and grabbed at her arm, catching it, he was able to twist her off him, as her flank was exposed, he delivered a strong punch to her kidney, jumped up and started to kick her ribs. She turned and grabbing his foot, threw him back to the ground. He did not stay put however and rolled away and up into a crouch. They both leaped towards each other, grappling for a hold. Grim got one first and twisted them both to the ground, with him on top. He delivered two punches to her face before she could get her block up. When she did, she made a sudden dive and grabbed at his crotch. With is testicles in her hand she stopped the fight. With the extreme pain, his cock stood straight up, and she jumped onto it, opening her vagina in time to take him whole. "Move you sucker. Move, like you never fucked before, if you want to live." He did not need to be told twice and he delivered a vicious fuck, which achieved what Nsonowa intended; they both began to shine with a blue/white fire. "Okay, get the fuck out of me." He did. "Get dressed, pick up your spear." He did. "Get out to your men. Skewer the first man who looks at you, that will fix the energy in your spear. Have every man touch his spear, sword, knife, whatever, to yours. Then put your troops in formation. Now go!" She practically threw him out of the tent, then donned her royal robes, in time to acknowledge Ugly who was supervising the deposition of the royal corpses into the tent. "Who is he, Ugly?"

"He is king Necor of Elutheria, the kingdom you have just taken your Majesty." She inspected his body. "Where is his royal seal, Ugly?"

"I took it for safekeeping, your Majesty."

"Give it to me!"

"Your Majesty, it goes to your privy council."

"I am my privy council, have you forgotten, now hand it over!" Ugly quickly did so, he had not forgotten. Nsonowa looked carefully at the seal. It was heavy, solid gold. It was stamped on one side with a likeness of the dead king, the other side, curiously, was stamped with an eagle in flight, lightning bolts clutched in it claws. She closed her eyes and pressed the seal to her forehead. And went rigid. In her mind flashed visions of slaughter, torture, rape and pillage. Her troops were doing the killing. She watched as the king's family was butchered in front of him, and then as Ugly himself was called up by Capitani and handed a knife with which he cut the kings throat. "Okay, Ugly. Why did we do this?"

"On your orders, your Majesty."

"And Why did we do this, Ugly?"

"For their gold, your Majesty."

"And do we have it now?"

"Yes, your Majesty."

"And where would it be now, Ugly?"

"As you speak, your Majesty, it is being loaded onto the freight wagons."

"Oh good, well we are going to walk over there and watch the loading. Anyone caught pilfering will lose their hands."

"Yes, your Majesty."

"Ugly. Where are we fighting next?"

"Why, your Majesty, you certainly kno...."

"Answer my question Ugly and you keep your head."

"Yes, your Majesty. We are marching north to take on Rufescent the Dark lord's consort."

"Ah, so. That's why I am here.." And she left the tent to move to the troops standing in formation.

"Capitani, call them to attention." He did and instantly five thousand men stood straight and raised their spears towards Nsonowa. "Heil to the King!" was lustily shouted repeated until Nsonowa held her own staff high and sent a blast of blue white fire towards the heavens.

"You have been given a bit of my magic. You will be victorious. Not one of you will fall. Slaughter all who oppose you. Harm none who yield. Bring me the witches head. General, give the order to march." And with that she collared Ugly and walked over to the supply wagons. "Which ones hold the gold.?" And having seen them, she pointed her staff at the drivers and ordered them to move these to her command tent. She followed them and once there, she bade them disembark and run double-time to catch up with the legions.

"Ugly, stand there." She made a gesture with her hands, and Ugly went rigid. She then went over to the corpses of the royal family. She put the seal on the dead king's chest. She made hand gestures and then touched the king with her staff, following with similar moves over his family. They woke. Amazed of course. Speechless.

"What have you done to us?" came from Necor the late King of Elutheria. "First you slaughter us, now what, are we to be zombie slaves? Haven't we suffered enough? Who are you?"

"I am Kalish Katlego Nsonowa, Chief of all Maasai, head Il'oi-bonokoh of the Black Sisterhood. And I don't make slaves, I free slaves, as I have freed you and your people from death. You'll find your treasure outside, intact. I am sorry for the terrors you have suffered, but I am not the one who did it. Ugly, over there, is primarily responsible and I am leaving him in your care. Please treat him with the respect he deserves. My troops have gone to fight some real evil on the other side of your land, the Darkside and its evil witch Rufescent. I shall not return." Then pounding her staff on the floor, she vanished in front of their astonished eyes.

###

21

Trio.

Nsonowa was clearly agitated. They had been discussing what Nsonowa had discovered while in the Mikvah.

"No! You two are NOT going. This is mine. And it will tax me and that is exactly what I want to happen, to keep my edge. And I don't want to have to worry about you two."

Flora was practically in tears, "Nsonowa, my beloved. I want to be there if you are in danger."

"Flora dear, your being there will increase her danger. Nsonowa, I am glad you have discovered the whereabouts of Rufescent. She is a horrible adversary. Sounds like so far, you have been on top of your game."

"Thank you, sir. and for me it seems like a golden opportunity. I get to fight so that you two lovebirds can have some uninterrupted connect time. Nothing could motivate me more. And, perhaps you two can help me help you by beaming me a steady stream of golden light energy. I am going to be burning up a lot of my blue-white light stores. Lilly and Ol'oi-boni will be my partners in generating more and sending it to the weapons, but that won't nourish my heart. That takes our golden light."

"Thank you, sister. That feels right, right from your heart to ours. It will be our pleasure and will motivate us to solve the problem of our communication from the cognitive side."

Flora spoke up through her tears, saying, "Yes, really thank you Nsonowa. We will do our part here. Our love will, literally, go with you. Goodbye, we will be in touch. House! See that Nsonowa has everything she needs for her trip." And with that the trio hugged, tightly hugged and cried together. They have had to battle separately before, but never separated by parallel realities. Nsonowa broke the circle and headed to the bath. "House. Hold the water temp constant and inject the nano probes. When you detect our location, transfer my material and weapon list." And she was gone. Stan and Flora kept up the hug. "Honey let's get to the bedroom and, suddenly Stan took off, waving to Flora as he left mindscape for a call back to his home in Los Angeles. It was much later when he returned.

"So why did you do that?" was what Flora wanted to know when he returned to her, in the cloud house.

"My timing sucks, that was my dinner obligation. I couldn't have not picked a worse time to open this conversation."

"And what was behind that choice my dearest?"

"I was impatient to start on this adventure. Once again, my impatience has gotten the best of me. You know, I don't like the way that sounds. I am the impatient one, there is no 'it" upon which to blame it."

"And, what was behind your impatience that doesn't want to be blamed?" was Flora's insightful question.

"I was afraid that I..... doesn't matter what it was. Fear is a thing in itself. I gave in to my feelings of fear. Now, how are those fears connected to our sexual relationship?"

Flora was quick with; "That problem won't be solved by talking it to death. I think we should make it to the bedroom and make love and see what comes up. Then we might see the answer to our vexing problem. Shall we?"

And the two wannabe lovebirds headed off to the bedroom, where they had recently functioned well sexually as a trio, raising the golden light with their three-way intercourse. Neither wanted any further interruptions, as they would also cause, not only the lost opportunity for joy, but also weaken Nsonowa in her struggle with Rufescent. Stan was aware of the stakes, "Precious time, precious time" lost for loving. He took Flora by the arm, gently leading her away and onto the bed. "First, darling. Let's destroy all of the clocks and live each moment."

"You don't have to ask me twice!" She jumped up and literally danced around the room flicking a hither-to unseen multitude of clocks, from off the walls, went into her closet, emerging in a negligee that brought Stan's eyes to the fore with a snap. She threw herself on top of the bed and laughing out "Come on in the water's fine."

Stan burst into a song; You are so Beautiful, on the way down. And he did go down, on her. With a wide opened mouth and heart, he consumed her genitals. He memorized instantly the glories of her exposed lady-parts, how her black pubic air framed her genital, and provided a beautiful border for her pink labia. He tasted the nectar with which she quenched his thirst for her. She began to giggle and squirm, then pulled him by his ears up to her face and began to kiss him, lustily. They both fell into the kiss so deeply, he hardly noticed when she piloted his now very engorged organ into her body. When she began to grind, he noticed. She gripped him fiercely with both her hands and her well lubricated tender vaginal linings, bringing him ever deeper into her. They both were moaning softly and when she began to feel his orgiastic energy rise, she slowed her movements and relaxed her vagina. He knew what she was doing and pulled part way out of her and positioned his head to look deeply into her eyes. What he saw startled him. What he saw, she expected, sadly. He saw the reflection of his own soul, that she knew would be there. What was reflected? The nasty smirk of Rufescent's spite gleaming at him through his mother's face. They were playing cards. An iconic game of the fifties and sixties called, wait for it, "Spite and Malice". That was all. That one image lodged deep in Flora's psyche, put there by Stan himself. As he watched, breathlessly, the image transformed in a transition so subtle you would not notice until it was complete. An image of Kali, the destroyer. A Dakini transform. Gleaming at him.

"Flora, you knew this?"

"Yes, my darling, it is a part of me. You are my creator. You gave me both sentience and sapience, so, yes, I know. Can you still love me? All of me?" and the question hung in the air between them like a poisonous cloud.

###

Nsonowa hit the ground running. She was late for her morning class, freshman magic. She wanted to stop by the residence and grab Lilly and Ol'oi-boni, but there would be no time. She was aware that should she be late on her first day, she would set the pattern for the term and her students would be a surely bunch. She visualized her battle clothing; she had added some very high-tech armor in unlikely places and put on her war-paint and burst into the classroom with a screech that would curdle the blood of the most seasoned warrior. The class was transfixed with terror. Several students fainted, she repeated the cry, And again. By the third time, some of the students began to relax. Two of them, a man and a woman, turned to tend to the fainted ones. In a 'normal' voice she said, "Take your seats, please." And to the pair attending the fallen, "I doubt they are seriously hurt. If you just prop them up in their chairs, we can get going."

A smart mouthed boy from the back of the room, called out, "You must mean 'coming' like in coming to, not going." She, wordlessly, pointed her spear at him, activated its laser and interfered with the gravity waves about him, sending him floating four feet above the class. "You, white boy, are 'coming' up front" and she drew him towards her. When he reached eye-level she undid his belt and grabbed his genitals as his pants fell off. "And now you are 'coming' all over yourself." as she jerked him into the act. He flushed an intense crimson and fell to the floor as she switched the laser off. "Get back to your seat." He drew a lot of sideways glances and a few snickers. She pointed to those doing the snickering, "You three, how did you get out of orientation? No, I am serious, tell us. What did you do to find the path out of orientation?" None of the three answered, and without batting an eye, she blasted them with the same laser, this time with violet light, and they disappeared with a popping sound.

"That's their transport back to orientation. Okay, class. What happened here? First one with the right answer is guaranteed to survive today's session." Several students started talking at once. "Okay, stop! You are just babbling. All of you take out your notebooks and pencils. Give me a thousand words describing what you saw. The one which has no spelling errors gets the guarantee." And with that she turned and bolted from the room.

She found Ol'oi-boni drinking coffee in the breakfast room. "Where's Lilly?" She demanded.

"Hey, that gal is intense. She woke, fondled me into a giant of an erection, and before I could grab her, she got off just looking at me, got out of bed and yelled back that she was on her way to the gym for a morning workout. So here I am with no gal to share this tool with.

"We can get to it soon enough, finish your coffee. I need to call Lilly. I'll meet you in the Mikvah after that."

"What's this Mikvah thing?"

"The bath, you can't miss it, it's this way." She headed to the bathroom. She needed a shower and would use the hot shower to call Lilly to her, then Join Ol'oi-boni in the bath and work up a charge of their blue-white energy. She shed her costume as she stepped into a frosted glass shower enclosure. Seven shower heads covering from the crown to the root blasted her with very hot, steaming hot, water. She took in the heat until she was ready to burst with its' energy, then sitting down on the teak bench she put her left hand into her en-gwali, (vagina in the Maasai language) and slowly began to rub. After a long time and gasping with the energy, she called to Lilly, "Come home, it's time". From the hot shower, she dunked herself into an icy bath from which she leapt out and called to Ol'oi-boni. "Hey bro, if you still have that erection, let's get started, and you can be less intimidating by the time Lilly gets here."

Lilly was working out with Bruce Lee, her martial arts coach. They were in the gym named after him. Bruce had just made one too many moves on her when Nsonowa's call came. She gave him a jab in his privates which put him away, turned and ran towards their res. She found herself running against a strong, cold, wet wind. It's started she thought, Damn, I wanted more time to prepare. I'll bet Nsonowa does too. She bundled her coat around her and ran even faster.

The weather had deteriorated further by the time she reached the others. She plunged into the now piping hot Mikvah, an antidote to the chill she had gotten right through her coat.

"Hey gal, you just in time." Growled Ol'oi-boni pushing them both to the surface where he impaled her anally on his now somewhat smaller, but never-the-less enormous organ. She gasped, and he moved her up and opened her legs to Nsonowa, who wasted no time in getting her tongue into Lilly's mound of Venus. Lilly lasted for about three seconds before her climax exploded into a searing blue-white light. It was radiating from her entire body and into both Nsonowa and Ol'oi-boni. There it was amplified three-fold and when the three of them were all glowing with an intensity that dissolved the Mikvah, the house, the reality and left them on the shore of a black-water lake.

It was a high mountain lake and the granite around them offered no shelter, nor did the dwarfed trees, blown over on their sides by a fierce wind. The shock stunned them for a second, before Nsonowa said, "quick, dive!" and plunged into the black water. When they emerged, they were covered by thick dense furred pelts. They huddled by the shore while Nsonowa told them why they were there. She wanted to leave immediately to find her army. They had been easily impressed by her authority when she took over the body of their marauding, murdering king and his council. Whether or not they would stay that way after her absence and restoration of all they had pillaged was another story. She would require strong magic and she hoped that Lilly and Ol'oi-boni would be up to it. She hoped that Stan and Flora could keep their spirits energized from the cloud house on mindscape.

"Nsonowa, there is a path down onto the plains where we are more likely to find them. I see no signs of any one person much less an army."

"Thanks, Ol'oi-boni. Lead." Which he did. They were running, partially to get to the army and partially to get out of the severe weather.

Ol'oi-boni, spotting the army first, approached, yelling in triumph. "We are here, Brothers. Dark fights with light, not against it."

"AIIIIIIIIII" Nsonowa let out her banshee screech leaping into the front of the army. "General Capitani! And she set off a blast of her blue-white lasers. The march stopped in its tracks. General Capitani rushed forward. "Yes Majesty."

They had won their army back. They still recognized her authority. "General, order a bivouac here. We must talk and plan." The General turned and began hollering out orders. The three fur-clad magicians entered the command tent where they shed their furs like stepping out of their skins. Nsonowa went to the desk of bones, Lilly and Ol'oi-boni took places on each side of her. Nsonowa wore her golden slave collar, ten inches thick covering her long and supple neck. She was covered in what looked like metal skin of pure gold. General Capitani knocked and entered. He was attended by five very strong warriors, dressed in their fiercest warpaints, and armed to the teeth with laser tech, Capitani had done well with the charge that Nsonowa had left him with. He looked forward to another session.

"Majesty, I am glad you are here. Some of the men began to grumble. I know they want a re-charge. As do I."

Capitani had a grin on his face that lasted until Ol'oi-boni grinned back and approached him, "Ask and you shall receive brother" Capitani was not grinning when Ol'oi-boni grabbed him, bent him over the desk of bones and proceeded to deliver the charge with a searing blast of blue-white energy deep into his ass. "Now bro, that should get those soldiers going again."

Capitani was trying to preserve his dignity, pulling up his pants, while looking to Nsonowa, Majesty, and asking where they were headed.

"There are caves in the granite mountains on the eastern edge of the plain where we might find her. I expect her defenses to be hidden in the foothills. Head straight for them. Ol'oi-boni is going to draw them out to you. I expect you to slaughter them all. Lilly," to whom she then pointed, "and I will, find and engage Rufescent. I expect support from all of you so don't dally with your job. When the field is cleared look for a red smoke in the mountain. That is where we will be."

Capitani left and began to rally his troops. Ol'oi-boni asked "How do you propose to get me to the foothills before the troops arrive?"

"We will fly, of course. Set up the ritual Lilly, I can give you class credit for it. Not you Ol'oi-boni, it's Magic 202. You're in 101." She chuckled and sat down on the desk to watch her student, her lover, and her new man in town, take positions on one of the carpets in the tent. Lilly put her hands over her butt. "I want to be on top Ol'oi-boni, I haven't quite recovered from our last fuck."

"Okay with me gal, you take it on" and he went down on his back, inviting Lilly to begin. She did, taking a cunnilingual/fellatio stance over his prostrate body. She took his engorged organ in both of her hands and put his fully exposed glans into her mouth. She gripped it with her tongue and began to chant from deep inside her. Soon both were humming and shining. The light from their bodies was penetrating the carpet. It began to float and shimmer. Lilly slowly pulled Ol'oi-boni still engorged, organ from her mouth and stood up coming down on him. "Hold still, I want to cap this off." and she resumed a grind that soon had the carpet supercharged.

"Jump aboard Sister. We are flying" Nsonowa did and a spit second later they erupted from the tent and flew like a rocket up and circling around the now moving army, jetted off towards the east.

Moments later they were making vulture like circles over the foothills, looking for possibilities for ambush. They spotted plenty of such. Rufescent had well covered her ass. She had known of the invasion ever since her spies told her of the Eleutherian King's defeat and the subsequent troop movements. She was confused by what was happening as Majesty of Eluthera was a sort-of ally. And wouldn't think of attacking her. He knew her strength, it would be suicide for him to try it. Even if he wanted to King Necro of the light side would stop him. And yet, here he was invading, and worse, she discovered, was he had some new power source. She had her army of ghouls and demons on high alert and setting up very nasty surprises for His Majesty.

Nsonowa directed their carpet to fly high enough to become invisible to those below. "It will be dark soon." She spoke to Ol'oi-boni, "I will land this thing and you take off. I suggest that you attack them just before dawn. Capitani should be arriving about then. You must have those ghouls hot on your heels by dawn."

"Oh, I am sure I can achieve that, I am so charged that...well, I don't know what.... but charged enough for that rabble. After we rout them what do you want from me?"

Lilly popped up with; "I know what I want!" and Nsonowa swatted her head.

"What you're going to get little one, is everything you can handle and then more, from Rufescent. You're staying with me. We are going in after her. Ol'oi-boni, get to us as soon as you can. We will need your help."

"How will I know where you have gone once you get into the mountain?"

"Follow the red smoke! Let's go down. Hold on everyone." And she put the carpet into a ninety-degree nose-dive. Reducing its visibility to any 'watchers' Rufescent might have still out. She pulled it out sharply to hover a few feet from the bottom of a wide gully. "Okay. Get this done for us." Ol'oi-boni jumped off the carpet, and Nsonowa and Lilly took off straight up and silently leaving Ol'oi-boni watching them go, somewhat wistfully. The power that he got from the two of them was over-the-top and possibly addicting. Wakanda with all its glories and achievements, never had developed this magic between the sexes. It was a testament to the complete openness of Nsonowa and Lilly. Maybe I do have something to learn at Safe Haven. No point being stubborn and insisting that I already know it all!

###

Stan began to breathe again and felt able to address Flora's question, "Now that I see Rufescent hiding out in my own soul, I can. The only way she can hurt me will be if I cut off my own nose."

"Silly one! Don't do that. You'll need it to sniff out her poison. And besides, I like it when you use it to rub my rose. Why wait? Let's get going." and she pulled her darling Stan's ears, moving his head down once again between her legs, opening again her labial rose petals giving access to his hungry tongue. Soon he was using his finger to massage her bud from the inside. She came, practically flooding him with her juices. She tightened her legs around his head and pulled him even harder into her tender parts. "Ohhhhhh...." and she began to shine. Stan heard her sigh and drank deeply of her climaxing juices, then pulled her legs apart and moved her hands, with his ears still tightly gripped, up her body until he once again was looking into her eyes. Once again, he entered her body from below and her soul from above. Their hearts beat in unison. Their breathing was reciprocal, and their souls flew, tuning and soaring into the celestial light. They were one with the one. They were all light. Flora's Dakini spirit took them home, into the light. Softly they came back. Back in the bed they couldn't get enough of looking at each other. Into their eyes, at their bodies, into their souls. They were love; they could see it. They could feel it. They could beam it out to search for Nsonowa.

###

Ol'oi-boni stood high on a knoll. His back was to the night of the western sky. The hills in front of him were in the shadow cast by the granite cliffs ahead, granite that housed Rufescent, an implacable enemy. A witch fed on human spite, a potent poison which gave her the power to kill many unsuspecting innocents. He knew what to do. He would survive this (he hoped). He was charged and ready to go. With a great scream he sent a blast of blue-white light, millions of degrees centigrade with the intensity of an exploding star, out across the hills in front of him. It burned off the tops of hills and crashed against the cliffs in the distance creating massive avalanches and a great earthquake that raced back into the foothills where it would sure wake the dead ghouls who were lying in ambush. When the earth stopped shaking, he again screamed a scream of angry defiance and blasted his light skyward creating a daytime which showed him off to the ghouls who were beginning to realize that they were under attack. Another blast and another scream, he knew would draw them out and to him. He turned and looked to the west from where he hoped Capitani's army would be when he got there. He delivered his last taunt, as the ghoulish horde began to rush his way.

###

Nsonowa and Lilly had timed their arrival to the granite cliffs to coincide with the blast they knew would come with the dawn. It did and when the rock and the dust settled, they flew up the cliff face until they saw the exposed opening to what looked like a large cave. The rock face was covered with blood, red blood. Nsonowa blasted it with her laser turning it to red smoke. How many were taken out by the avalanche? Hopefully enough to give them a chance to land and establish a beachhead. Lilly was the lookout, Nsonowa was pilot, she hovered just below the floor of the cave and Lilly looked over the edge and motioned to lower the rug. "There are about a hundred of the demons milling about, I couldn't see a trace of the witch."

"Hold on honey." And with that she flew away, up, and sped full on into the cave burning everything in the cave to ash with the laser. "Off now!" Lilly jumped onto the cave floor, and Nsonowa joined her, then sent the carpet to hover just outside the cave mouth, where they might be jumping for their lives. "Come on honey. Let's find the bitch."

"You've already found her!" words said with a nasty laugh boomed from above them. And a huge part of the cave ceiling collapsed onto Nsonowa, leaving Lilly standing looking in horror at the boulder occupying the space that a second before had contained her friend and lover. The shock, which might have paralyzed her, put her into motion, she positively flew around the cavern locating Rufescent by her stench. She screamed Nsonowa's battle cry and threw herself on top of the witch. She held her head in her hands and ripped it from the neck of the hag, whom she turned over and ripping off her rags, stuffed the startled head into her ass. She turned to the pile of rocks and began to move them starting with the biggest first and putting the whole of the stored blue-white light into her effort lifted the rock off the crushed body of her friend. Seeing her bleeding and broken body almost broke her heart and she collapsed in tears and grief. She hadn't begun to catch her breath when she was picked up from behind by the strong arms of Ol'oi-boni. "Link with me Lilly." And he entered her and began to pump creating a pulse of light. "It's not enough" she cried. "We need help. Oh my god, sister come back." Ol'oi-boni increased his efforts. Nsonowa had stopped gushing blood, but there was no other movement. Both began to despair. Then Lilly grabbed Ol'oi-boni. "No, I won't let us lose her." We need more help. Turn around, and in a repeat of an earlier effort at fellatio soon produced a blast of the blue-white light which shone out of the cave drawing Stan and Flora's golden love light from source.

The cave dissolved from the intensity generated by the love of the four of them. They were in the Mikvah back in the residence on Safe Haven. Nsonowa was just coming to.

"She was horrible!" she croaked out.

"and she met a horrible end," was Lilly's rejoinder.

Stan and Flora smiled at each other. Stan said, "Nsonowa, have you had enough adventure for a while?"

"This was just a taste of what I want. And we still have a job to do back on Safe Haven. One that is going to take both Lilly's and Ol'oi-boni's energies. Besides, I want to be part of their graduation ceremonies, when they pass their classes, of course."

"You are one tough teacher, lady!" came from Ol'oi-boni, and Lilly chimed in with, "a lot more tender than you Ol'oi-boni! And don't you ever get tender, either."

Flora, with a huge smile asked if they could have one more go around in the tub before the three took off. "A daisy chain would be nice" and she batted her long lashes with a very mischievous grin on her face.

"I think I might sit that one out." Said Lilly.

"I didn't think you could sit." Quipped Ol'oi-boni, and besides, I want some of Flora. "Beautiful, you look delicious."

"Thank you, I think I would like some of you too."

Stan chirruped in with, "Lilly I have read a lot about you, I would love to get to know you from the inside, so to speak." Lilly answered with sparkling eyes and a flip of her skirt.

Nsonowa gave her a quick elbow and added; "I'm volunteering to be in the center of this chain, I could use the healing energy." and with giggles and sighs, the tulpas, their host, Stan, and the Safe Haven magicians, proceeded to say a loving and healing goodbye in the beautiful blue tiled Mikvah.

finis

Printed in Great Britain
by Amazon

64860684R00109